Statue of evil . . .

A cloud passed overhead. Michael felt a chill as he stared up at the gargoyle. He'd always hated the ugly thing. The statue perched at the top of the gable on the third-floor roof. It had a twisted face that was half-dog and half-monkey. It's deadly-looking claws poked out beneath pointed, batlike wings. And it sat up there and leered down at anyone who entered the house, ready to fly off the roof and dig in its talons and—

"What the . . ." Michael murmered as he stared at the statue. He could have sworn that the gargoyle had moved. *No, couldn't have*, he muttered to himself. But he'd definately seen something. What was going on?

Michael blinked and squinted. There it was again. There *was* something up there . . .

Be sure not to miss
these other Trophy Chillers:

Night of the Gargoyle

Gargoyle

LLOYD ALAN

HarperTrophy

A Division of HarperCollins*Publishers*

HarperCollins®, ▆®, and A Trophy Chiller®
are trademarks of HarperCollins Publishers Inc.

Night of the Gargoyle
Copyright © 1995 by Parachute Press, Inc.

1 2 3 4 5 6 7 8 9 10
❖
First Harper Trophy Edition

CHAPTER 1

Michael Buckner knelt on the edge of the gym mat and raised a hand to push his hair off his forehead. Across from him, Tucker Tropowsky squatted on the other side of the mat, grinning nastily.

It was only his second day of karate lessons and already things were going badly. At first, Michael had been really excited about taking the after-school class. He and his best friend Max Morris had talked about nothing else for days. They couldn't wait to learn all the fancy chops and kicks they'd seen in a million action movies. But Michael didn't know that Tucker Troposwky would be taking the class, too.

Tucker was bigger than Michael. He was bigger than any of the eleven-year-old boys in their fifth-grade class at Lakeview Middle School. Bigger and stronger. And definitely meaner.

Tucker was Michael's least favorite person in the whole school. In all of Lakeview, for that

1

matter. Maybe in the whole world. Tucker was always giving Michael a hard time. The only time he'd stopped was when Michael had written an English essay for him. After that, Tucker had left Michael alone—for about three weeks. Then Tucker had gone back to being a bully. And now Mr. Dooley, the karate teacher, had made Michael and Tucker sparring partners in class.

Max kept telling Michael he had nothing to worry about. After all, Max told him, karate taught little guys how to defend themselves against big guys like Tucker.

"Yeah," Michael had agreed. "But what if the big guys are learning the same moves as the little guys?"

Max had no answer to that.

"Okay, people, let's try it again." Mr. Dooley clapped his hands together and paced along the back of the gym. He held out his hands and showed them to the class. His fingers were pointed straight out, palms flat.

"Okay. No fists," he said. "In this move, the hands must be open. Empty."

"Yeah, empty—just like your head, Buckner," Tucker murmured. It was just loud enough for Michael, Max, and everyone near them to hear. A couple of the guys snickered.

"Cut it out, Tropowsky," Michael warned.

"Who's gonna make me?" Tucker smirked.

Michael shook his head. It was just his luck to

be paired with the king of the jerks.

"Now imagine that your mind is a pond," Mr. Dooley was saying. He made a big circle with his hands. "The water in the pond is quiet and still. You must make your mind as still as the pond."

"I'd like to dunk you in a pond, Buckner," Tucker hissed. "Headfirst."

Michael tried to ignore him. Next to Michael, Max sighed and rubbed a hand over his close-cropped red hair. "Lamebrain," Max muttered. Michael laughed.

Mr. Dooley paced toward the other side of the gym. "When you practice karate, all anger must leave you," Mr. Dooley said. He glanced around the room and nodded in approval at the boys and girls assembled there. "Looks good. Now you can try those chops and kicks I showed you. But remember, don't connect! We're not here to—"

Before Mr. Dooley could finish, Michael saw Tucker's closed fist aiming straight at his face.

"Duck!" Max yelled.

Michael jumped to one side. Tucker's fist connected with Michael's shoulder. Michael grunted in pain. He looked up just in time to see Tucker lift his right leg. He sent a high kick straight toward Michael's stomach.

Michael jumped out of the way again. This time Tucker's foot hit the side of Michael's leg.

Mr. Dooley saw it all. "Tucker Tropowsky!" he yelled across the room. "Didn't you hear a word

I said?" The teacher ran to Tucker's side.

Michael and Max exchanged looks of satisfaction. Tucker was really going to get it now.

Mr. Dooley reached Tucker and grabbed his hand. "No fists, I said! The hand must be open and empty." He forced Tucker's hand out flat.

That's it? Michael's mouth dropped open. He couldn't believe his eyes! Tucker had tried to clobber him. And now he was getting away with it!

"Now shake hands," Mr. Dooley told Tucker.

Tucker hesitated. Then he stuck out his hand. Michael had no choice, not with Mr. Dooley and the whole class watching them. He shook hands with the bully. He could see the message in Tucker's eyes: just wait till next time.

You wait, Tropowsky, Michael thought. *Next time I'll be ready.*

After karate class Michael and Max walked home in silence. They both lived on Moonlight Drive. When they reached the end of the driveway that led up to Michael's house, a big golden retriever bounded up to them. The dog barked and jumped all over them, trying to lick their hands.

"Hiyah, Gruff," Michael greeted his dog. "Hiyah, fella." Michael turned to Max and grinned. "Looks like Gruff wants you to come over," he said.

"Sorry." Max shook his head. "Can't. Too much homework. Besides, I'm worn out from karate. I don't have the strength to face the House of Horrors today."

"House of Horrors" was one of Michael's many nicknames for his home. *Casa del mondo creepioso* was another. Its real name was Moonlight Mansion, and it stood on the top of the biggest hill in Lakeview, looming over all the other residences on Moonlight Drive. Old and gloomy, it looked just like something out of one of the horror movies Michael liked to watch.

The mansion had been built over two hundred years ago. It had belonged to Grammy Rose, Michael's grandmother, until recently. Then Grammy had moved to Florida and left the house to Michael's family. Michael and his older sister, Sara, hadn't wanted to move there. But their parents couldn't wait. Mr. and Mrs. Buckner adored the house—but then, most adults did. They never saw the things that Michael and Sara and other kids did. They had no idea that there was evil in Moonlight Mansion.

Like the monster that attacked them in the graveyard on Halloween. And the baby-sitter who had seemed so nice . . . until she'd tried to control Michael and his sister with evil dolls.

And the ghost.

The ghost of Elizabeth Carter had been the

worst thing they'd faced so far. It had almost tricked them into destroying themselves. Sara and Michael had stopped it just in time—and had learned something important.

A man named Jonah Carter had owned the house long ago. He had created the evil in Moonlight Mansion. Now Michael and Sara were determined to fight Jonah and destroy the evil— if it didn't destroy them first.

"Catch you later, Buckner," Max called as he hurried down the street to his own house.

Michael watched his friend go. He didn't blame Max for not wanting to come in. Max had been Michael's friend long enough to have seen the evil himself—and to have been attacked by it, too. Sighing, Michael turned up the long, winding driveway. As he neared the front door, he stared up at the house and frowned. If only it didn't *look* so creepy. If only it didn't have those steep-sloped gables and that pointy tower in one corner. And that brass door knocker that was shaped like a serpent, coiled up to strike. And most of all, that awful stone gargoyle.

A cloud passed overhead. Michael felt a chill as he stared up at the gargoyle. He'd always hated the ugly thing. The statue perched at the top of the gable on the third-floor roof. It had a twisted face that was half-dog and half-monkey. Its deadly-looking claws poked out beneath pointed, batlike wings. And it sat up there and leered down at anyone who entered the house, ready to fly off the roof and dig in its talons and—

"What the . . ." Michael murmured as he stared at the statue. He could have sworn that the gargoyle had moved. *No, couldn't have,* he muttered to himself. But he'd definitely seen something. What was going on?

Michael blinked and squinted. There it was again. There *was* something up there . . .

"Dad!" Michael yelled in relief. Mr. Buckner stepped out from behind the statue and waved down at him.

"Hey, Michael," his father called. "Ready to help fix the shingles?"

Michael gulped. His dad had told him to hurry home from practice so he could help fix the roof. He had forgotten all about it.

"Uh, sure," Michael yelled back. "All set." He hurried closer to the mansion. "What should I do?" he called.

Mr. Buckner held up a shingle. "I'm replacing the loose ones. They come off pretty easily. I'll toss them down, and you stack them up for me, okay?"

"Okay," Michael said.

Michael watched as his dad bent over and began working. The first few shingles lifted off right away. Michael gathered them up into a neat pile and waited for his dad to throw down some more.

The next one gave Mr. Buckner more trouble. He bent lower and grabbed it with both hands. Michael watched as his dad braced his foot against the roof, leaned back, and pulled up hard on the stubborn shingle. All at once, the shingle came loose. Mr. Buckner stumbled and lost his balance.

"Watch out, Dad!" Michael yelled in sudden fear. He took a step toward the house, keeping his eyes pinned on his father. "Don't fall, don't fall," he muttered anxiously.

Mr. Buckner threw himself backward—right into the gargoyle. "Oomph!" he grunted.

Michael winced. *That must've hurt*, he thought. *But at least Dad's all right . . . What was that?*

A strange, rumbling noise—almost like a low groan—came from overhead.

Michael stared up at the roof. For an instant, the gargoyle seemed to lean over and leer right into Michael's face.

"Michael!" his father screamed.

Michael froze in shock. The gargoyle wasn't leaning over. It was falling. And it was headed right toward him.

CHAPTER 2

"Michael! Get out of the way!" Mr. Buckner shouted.

Michael moved just in time. The gargoyle fell past him so closely that he could feel an icy draft as it flew by. It crashed onto an old yew bush that was so huge it cushioned the fall.

"Michael—are you all right?" Mr. Buckner raced down the ladder and ran to his side. "That was way too close."

"Yeah," Michael murmured. "I know."

Mr. Buckner leaned over the gargoyle. "I must have knocked it loose when I bumped into it," he said. He shaded his eyes, gazing up at the blank space on the roof where the gargoyle had stood.

"I didn't think I bumped it that hard," Mr. Buckner remarked. "But I'd better go back and take a good look. Something must be loose up there."

Michael stared at the gargoyle lying on its

back in the yew bush, completely unharmed. It was almost as big as Michael. Its snakelike eyes stared upward. Its lips were drawn back in its usual sickly grin. Michael could have sworn it was laughing at him.

"Couldn't we, like, just get rid of it, Dad?"

"Get rid of it?" Mr. Buckner raised his eyebrows. "I know you kids don't like it. But it has historical value, Michael. That statue is worth a lot of money."

"I don't get it, Dad. It's so ugly."

"Just because something is ugly doesn't mean it isn't worth something. Besides, I kind of like it." Mr. Buckner shook his head thoughtfully. "No, we'll have to get it fixed. I wonder if we could move it."

Michael couldn't believe his ears. "Are you kidding? That thing must weigh a ton!"

"But I was able to knock it over," his father pointed out. "Maybe it isn't as heavy as it looks. Let's see if we can take it to the toolshed."

"If we *can* move it then it's probably a fake," Michael protested. "Made out of some discount rock or something." But his father wasn't listening. Michael sighed. He had no desire to touch the statue, but it looked as if he didn't have a choice.

Michael's dad bent over the gargoyle and grabbed hold of its clawed feet. "You take the top," he told Michael.

Michael crouched to get a grip on the gargoyle's arm. Gritting his teeth, he touched the stone—and immediately pulled his hands away. "Wow!"

Mr. Buckner looked annoyed. "Now what?"

"It's so cold," Michael explained. "Like touching ice cubes. Doesn't it feel cold to you?"

"Stone is always cool," his father said. "All right. Let's do this together. On three. One, two, three—"

They both lifted. Michael staggered under his half of the weight. Discount stone or not, the statue was heavy enough—so heavy that his knees nearly buckled. His father's face looked strained, too. "Holy cow!" Michael gasped.

"Take it easy, Michael," his dad said. "We'll go real slow."

It took them quite a while to get the statue into the toolshed and then to hoist it onto the worktable. The table was made of sturdy posts, braced with metal crosspieces underneath. Still, Michael expected the table to sag or even break under the weight of the gargoyle. But the table held firm.

"Whew." Michael wiped his brow. "I'm glad that's done."

His dad grinned. "Well, when I asked you to help with home improvements, I didn't have this in mind," he admitted.

"What'll we do now?"

Mr. Buckner examined the gargoyle closely. "I don't see any damage. But look here." His dad pointed to the bottom of the statue. Michael saw several large holes drilled around the gargoyle's feet.

Mr. Buckner rubbed his thumb around the holes. When he held up his hand, Michael saw some reddish dust on the end of his finger.

"What's that stuff?"

"Rust," Mr. Buckner answered. "There were bolts in here once. They held the statue to the base on the roof. The bolts must have rusted away somehow." He shook his head. "I'd better stop in town tomorrow. Maybe someone at the hardware store can tell me how to repair this."

"Maybe they'll find someone to do it for you," Michael suggested hopefully. *No way am I going to touch that thing again,* he thought. *Especially not to fix it.*

His father looked amused. "Come on, kid— this is a challenge! We should at least *try* to do it ourselves. Okay?"

Michael gave him a halfhearted smile. "Sure. Okay."

At that moment, Michael's mother called from the house. "Honey! Phone for you. It's your office. They said it's important."

"Close up in here, okay Michael?" Mr. Buckner sprinted into the house.

Michael gave a last look around the toolshed. Everything was in order. He turned to follow his father.

Suddenly, something reached out and grabbed him. Michael felt a sharp sting in his arm. He couldn't move. *It's the gargoyle*, he thought, panicking. *The gargoyle has me!*

Michael took a deep breath. Slowly, he glanced down at his side—and almost laughed. He had snagged his sweatshirt on the sharp talons of the gargoyle's claw.

I must be losing it, Michael thought. *I really thought that gargoyle grabbed me. Guess I've been living in the* casa del mondo creepioso *too long.*

Michael pulled his sweatshirt off the talons and pushed up his sleeve. He was bleeding. Tiny red drops beaded up along a jagged scratch on his arm.

Did the gargoyle scratch me on purpose? he wondered. After all, it was part of the house, and you never knew . . . *Get a grip, Buckner*, he told himself. Still, he made sure the shed door was shut firmly behind him before he went into the house.

After dinner, Michael hurried up to his room to finish his homework. He had a big paper on Central America due for social studies class. He was just starting to work when his older sister, Sara, came charging in with Gruff at her side.

"Have you ever heard of knocking?" Michael asked.

Sara ignored him.

"As long as you're here—what's the chief crop of Nicaragua?"

"How should I know?" Sara thought a minute. "Bubble gum."

"You're a big help," Michael complained.

Sara picked up Michael's mug and took a sip. "Yeccch!" She grimaced. "What *is* that?"

"Body Builder. It's a protein drink." Michael grinned at the expression on her face. "To bulk me up. You know, to add muscle."

"You're actually drinking that without anyone *making* you?"

"It's not so bad. You'd drink it too, if you were taking karate." *And staring across the mat at Tucker Tropowsky*, Michael added to himself.

"Did you learn anything yet?" Sara asked.

"Sure. I'll show you the whole routine." Michael began by stretching backward, forward, and sideways, and moved into some deep body bends. Then he demonstrated the basic karate chop and kick.

"Doesn't look like much," Sara remarked. "I thought karate was deadly."

"This punch is deadly," Michael said seriously. He made his hands as flat as he could and pretended to slash at an attacker's neck.

"Oh, right," Sara scoffed. "Who do you think you are? The next Bruce Lee?"

"Maybe. Here, wait a minute."

Michael spotted the board that had been kept under his old mattress for support. He propped it up between two chairs.

"Watch this, if you don't believe me."

He straightened his hand and raised his arm. They hadn't broken any boards in class yet. In fact, Mr. Dooley had told them to forget about stunts like that since they were only beginners.

Michael didn't intend to really *hit* anything. He was just fooling around.

Sara watched him with a sarcastic grin. "You're bluffing," she said.

"Oh, yeah?" She was right, but Michael didn't intend to let her know that—yet. He centered himself, his legs opened wide. "My mind is a pond." He squatted and bent both arms at the elbows. "It is quiet—" he held his arms out to his sides "—and still." He made his right hand as flat as he could, until it looked like the edge of a knife. Sara was still smirking, he saw. He inhaled, taking a long, slow breath. *Now*, he told himself.

"Eeiiaah!" Michael slashed his right arm down toward the board. It went a lot faster than he expected—so fast that there was no time to pull back, as he'd intended.

He couldn't stop!

He was going to smash his hand to bits!

CHAPTER 3

Michael's hand crashed into the board.

He stared down at the floor. The heavy piece of wood lay there in two pieces.

He had sliced the board in half!

"I don't believe it!" Sara cried. She gaped at the smashed board. "How did you do that?"

"Uh, it was easy," Michael fibbed. *Wow*, he thought to himself. *This karate stuff is cool!*

Michael examined his hand. It looked fine. No scratches, no bruises—nothing. *Wow.*

"Hey, what's that?" Sara pointed at Michael's bare arm.

The scratch he'd gotten earlier had healed into three jagged scabs. "Oh, that." Michael shrugged. "I scratched myself on that dumb gargoyle statue."

Sara nodded. "Yeah. I heard Dad knocked it off the roof." She made a face. "Too bad you can't smash *that* to smithereens."

Michael held up his hands. "Hmmm . . ."

"Don't even think about it." Sara giggled. "Mom and Dad would have a fit. You know they love that thing."

"I know," Michael agreed. "They are so weird."

"Well, I've got to go finish my homework," Sara said. Gruff scrambled to his feet and followed her to the door.

"Hey—" Michael called after her. "If you want me to break anything for you, just yell!"

Sara laughed as she went down the hall.

In the morning, Michael woke up and leaped out of bed. He found the boards just as he had left them the night before. Broken straight through. Clean as a whistle.

Michael grinned at himself in the mirror and held up his hands. *Licensed weapons*, he thought. *Yikes! Look at that!* he blinked.

His fingernails! When he went to sleep, they were normal, chewed up the way they always were. Now they were long. Extremely long. They had sprung out half an inch beyond the ends of his fingertips. And they looked sharp, too.

How could they grow like that in one night?

Michael raised a hand to his cheek. Very, very carefully he scratched himself. *Yeow!* His nails were really dangerous! His mouth dropped open in shock.

He glanced at himself in the mirror. *That's*

17

weird, he thought. His mouth was open pretty wide. He could imagine his mother coming in at any moment and yelling at him: "You better watch out or your face will freeze like that!"

Michael laughed to himself. Dumb. Your face couldn't freeze. He closed his mouth. Or tried to. It wouldn't move. He tried again. It didn't budge. His jaw was wide open—

And he couldn't get it to close!

This is crazy! Michael felt a stab of fear. His face was so *stiff.* In fact, now that he thought about it, he felt kind of stiff all over.

Michael tried to move his mouth again. Nothing. Now he was really starting to panic. He couldn't go to school looking like this. He looked like a . . . a pelican!

Maybe he was just a little tense. Michael tried to relax. *My mind is a pond,* he told himself. *It is quiet and still. I am calm. I can move my muscles. . . .*

Just like that, Michael's jaw closed. Carefully, he opened and closed his mouth a few times to make sure it was normal. It worked fine.

Michael glanced at his clock. The alarm hadn't gone off. He was going to be late for school if he didn't hurry. He threw on his clothes and hurried down the hall. The one good thing about being late was that he had the bathroom all to himself. He washed quickly and searched under the sink for a pair of nail clippers.

18

"Here we go," he muttered. "Goodbye, ugly nails." He held the clippers to his left thumbnail and squeezed. The nail bent slightly and sprang back. Was something wrong with the clippers? They didn't seem to be working. Michael tried again, squeezing them even harder. His nail wasn't even dented. He squeezed with all his might.

SNAP! A coil on the clippers sprang loose and flew across the room.

Holy cow! His nails were so hard they broke the clippers!

Michael hurried into Sara's room. She was even later than he was—she was just waking up. Gruff raised his head and looked at Michael from the foot of the bed where he was sleeping. He whimpered and tried to push his big nose into Michael's hands. Gruff always did that when he wanted to be petted.

"Not now, boy. Sorry. But I might scratch you."

Sara sat up and yawned. "Scratch him? What are you talking about?" she asked sleepily.

Michael held out his hands. His nails looked even longer than they had in the bathroom. Sara gasped, shocked into wakefulness. "Your nails!" she cried. "They're disgusting!"

Michael nodded grimly. "It happened while I was sleeping."

Sara whistled softly. "You better stop taking

19

that protein drink. That could make your nails grow, you know. Fingernails are all protein—at least, I think they are."

Michael held out the broken clippers. "I tried to cut them off, and look what happened!"

Sara examined the damage. "Wow. You ruined these, Michael."

"Who cares?" Michael said impatiently. "What about me? I look like a freak."

"Okay, don't panic." Sara thought for a moment. "I know!" She rushed to her desk drawer. "Gruff's nail clippers!"

But the pet clippers didn't work either.

Michael groaned. "Great. I'm gonna have to go to school wearing boxing gloves or something."

"Take it easy. I have another idea," Sara said. "You know our new veterinarian?"

"No. You're the animal lover, not me." That was true. His sister had an entire menagerie of pets in her room, including a hamster, two parakeets, and two goldfish. "How is that supposed to help me, Sara?"

"Just listen. He told me another way you could take care of animals' nails. If you can't clip them—file them!" Sara searched her drawer until she found a nail file. Michael grabbed it from her. He had trouble holding it at first—his nails got in the way—but at last he drew the file along the top of his longest fingernail. The thin file bent in half.

"Great." Michael threw the file on the floor. "I broke that too."

"You need a bigger file, that's all," Sara said.

Michael brightened. "There's a big one in the toolshed," he said hopefully. "If that doesn't work, nothing will!"

Michael waited impatiently while his sister got dressed. Then he raced down the stairs with Sara and Gruff close behind him.

"Hey, you two—breakfast," their father yelled. They rushed through the hall without stopping. "In a minute, Dad!" Michael yelled back. He and Sara hurried into the toolshed. Michael tried not to look at the gargoyle, but he found himself glancing at it anyway.

The statue looked just as it had when he had left it. Except . . . Michael leaned toward it. *Am I crazy or is that thing smirking at me?* he wondered. He scowled. *Dumb. Dumb.* He felt as if the gargoyle were watching him. Laughing at him. How he hated that stupid piece of rock!

"Hey, here's the toolbox," Sara called.

Michael rummaged through it and found the file.

"Let's do this outside," he told Sara. He had to get away from the gargoyle's leering face.

Outside the shed, he grasped the file tightly and held it to his nails.

Come on and work, he pleaded silently.

CHAPTER 4

Michael raked the big file across his fingernail. There was a raspy sound—and then bits of nail flew into the air. "Yes!" he shouted.

The file worked, but it was tough going. Michael and Sara had to take turns in order to finish all ten of Michael's nails. They barely had time to grab breakfast and catch a ride to school with their dad.

As soon as he could, Michael told Max all about how he broke the board the night before.

"Awesome," Max said as they headed down the hall to social studies.

"You should've seen Sara's face." Michael grinned.

"But how did you know how to do it?" Max asked. "We haven't learned anything like that yet."

"I don't know. I guess it's all in the timing."

They walked into the classroom, still talking. Their teacher, Mr. Morse, looked up at them and nodded hello. He was a nice guy, and Michael would have liked his class a lot. Except for one thing—Tucker Tropowsky. He was in the class, too. As Michael and Max entered, Tucker glanced up and sneered. Michael ignored him—as usual—and took his seat.

"Okay, class. Quiet down," Mr. Morse ordered. "Let's pick up where we left off yesterday. Central America."

There were a few groans. Michael groaned, too. He slid down in his seat. Today's class was going to be a long one.

Mr. Morse glanced at Michael and frowned. "Sit up, Michael," he said. Michael sat up. He knew what was coming next. Mr. Morse was a fitness nut. He was really into eating right, working out, and exercising. And he almost always started each class with a little lecture about health.

"That's better." Mr. Morse nodded in approval. "You know what I always say. Good posture is the key to good work. Good posture aligns your spine, and an aligned spine improves all of your brain functions. Cognition, memory, problem solving . . ."

Michael felt a big yawn coming on. He raised a hand to cover his mouth. *Ow.* His arms were really sore today. He'd better take it easy in karate later.

". . . treat your body right and it will treat *you* right," Mr. Morse continued.

Michael closed his mouth. Or tried to. *Oh,no!* he thought anxiously. His mouth was stuck— again! He sat bolt upright.

"Excellent, Michael." Mr. Morse smiled at him. "I see you've been listening."

Michael managed to nod at the teacher. Worriedly, he noticed a few kids glancing his way. Max was staring at him with a curious expression.

Michael grabbed his social studies book and held it up to his face to cover his open mouth.

Empty pond. Still water, Michael told himself frantically, but it didn't seem to help.

While Mr. Morse's back was turned, Max shoved a note at him.

What's wrong with your face?

Michael stared across the aisle at Max and pointed at his jaw behind his textbook. "Uck. Uck," he grunted. He was trying to say "stuck." Max stared at him intently.

"You kids don't give your spines a fighting chance," Mr. Morse was saying. "You abuse them. You're spine abusers."

Michael tried motioning to Max with his hand. *How do you motion that your jaw is stuck?* he wondered hysterically.

Mr. Morse had finished his health speech and had moved on to social studies. He tapped Judy Simpson on the shoulder. "Judy, what can you tell the class about the chief crops of Central America?"

"The chief staple of Central American agriculture is . . ." she began.

Michael shoved his hand up against the bottom of his chin. Maybe he could force his jaw shut.

Max saw what he was doing and let out a snort of laughter.

Mr. Morse frowned.

"Another important crop is the banana," Judy Simpson continued, "and jute. Jute is very important."

Michael raised his textbook higher with one hand and shoved his jaw again with the other. Really hard.

Max wasn't the only one who laughed this time. Tucker guffawed loudly. Mr. Morse turned around to see what was going on. He glared at Michael. Michael quickly lowered his head and pretended to be studying his book.

Mr. Morse's quiet voice was deadly. "Michael, perhaps you'd like to explain to the class what jute is?"

Talk about jute! He couldn't talk, period! He hadn't been able to move his mouth since practically the beginning of class! Desperately, he shook his head "no" and pretended to read some more.

"Michael? Do you think this is funny?" The teacher hovered over him.

Michael took a deep breath. He had to do something. He curled his fist into a tight ball and closed his eyes.

Then he punched himself in the jaw.

There was a gasp from the class. Someone snickered. Someone else let out a peal of nervous laughter.

"Michael!" Mr. Morse looked shocked.

But Michael's jaw snapped shut. He wiggled it back and forth—it worked! He spoke quickly. "Jute is . . . jute is . . . uh, a vegetable," he babbled. "Sort of like a tomato. Or like an onion—"

"Never mind," Mr. Morse cut him off. "Michael, I suggest you go home tonight and have lots of carbohydrates for dinner."

"Carbohydrates?"

"For energy," Mr. Morse replied. "You'll need a lot of it for the report you're going to write on jute. Three hundred words. By tomorrow, you'll be an expert on it. Got that?"

"Yes, sir," Michael murmured. "I've got it."

CHAPTER 5

Mr. Dooley walked to the front of the gym. "Okay, everyone. Settle down for a minute."

It was after school and Michael was back in karate class.

Mr. Dooley waited until he had everyone's attention. Then he put his hands together and bowed to the students. Michael, Max, and the rest of the class bowed back. Michael noticed that Tucker had a big smirk on his face when he bowed.

"In two weeks we have our first exhibition match," Mr. Dooley announced. There were some groans from the class. "I know, I know." Mr. Dooley grinned. "You're new at this. But don't worry. I'll get you ready in time. So let's get back to what we were doing. Anyone who needs extra help, raise your hand."

Tucker grabbed Michael's right arm and hoisted it into the air. "Me, sir, me!" he called in a high voice. "I need *lots* of extra help!"

Everyone laughed.

Michael tore his arm out of Tucker's grasp. "Not funny, Tropowsky," he snapped.

"Hey, everything about you is funny, Buckner." Tucker snorted. "Or should I call you Jute Boy?"

He swung back his fist and jabbed it into Michael's face.

"C'mon, Jute King," Tucker taunted.

"Get lost, Tucker," Michael warned.

"Oooh, I'm scared." Tucker pretended to tremble. "But not as scared as you were in Morse's class. You should've seen yourself today. 'Jute is, duh, like a tomato. Oh, please, Mr. Morse, don't yell at me!'" Tucker laughed uproariously.

Michael felt his face redden. "Cut it out, Tropowsky." He clenched his fist and drew back.

"Control, boys—control!" Mr. Dooley called from across the gym. "Remember, karate is all about discipline."

"Buckner knows about discipline," Tucker drawled. "When he's bad, he punches *himself* in the face!"

That's it, Michael told himself, enraged. He bent his head and charged. "Eeiiaah!" he screamed.

Tucker saw him coming and leaped out of the way. Michael plowed right into Max instead. His head caught Max in the stomach.

"Oomph!" Max toppled backward onto the mat. Michael landed on top of him.

For a moment, neither of them moved. "Sorry, Max," Michael managed to say. He drew in a shaky breath, pushed himself up, and sat next to his best friend. "Are you all right?"

Max was still lying flat on his back, his eyes wide open. He was staring at the ceiling as if he didn't know what had hit him.

Mr. Dooley rushed over to them. "Easy, Max. You just had the wind knocked out of you. Relax—take it slow and easy."

The panicked look started to leave Max's eyes.

"That's it," Mr. Dooley said.

Max drew in a shaky breath. Then another. Mr. Dooley helped him sit up before turning to Michael.

Michael could tell he was really angry. His voice shook a little when he started to speak. "*Discipline*, Michael," he said between gritted teeth. "*Control*. Karate is an art form. It is not a street fight. Understand?"

"Yes sir," Michael mumbled.

"Now you two bow to show respect," Mr. Dooley ordered.

Max got to his feet. He and Michael bowed to each other.

"Sorry, Max," Michael said again when Mr. Dooley had left them. "Are you okay?"

"Do I look okay?" Max took a few deep

breaths. He glanced up at his friend. Michael was smiling hugely. "What are you grinning at?"

"I was just thinking. I totally knocked you out by accident. A few more weeks of karate, and think what I could do to Tropowsky—on purpose!"

Max walked Michael to the end of his driveway.

"See you tomorrow. I can't wait to hear all about jute." Max grinned.

"You'll be staggered by all the information," Michael told him. "See you." He walked up the hill toward his house.

The sun was bright and the day was warm, but he still felt a chill as he approached the *casa del mondo creepioso*. At least the gargoyle wasn't there anymore, peering down at him with that twisted grin.

His dad was on the roof again. Michael yelled up a greeting. Mr. Buckner climbed down the ladder and hurried to meet him.

"What's up, Dad? Want more help with the shingles?"

Mr. Buckner shook his head. "No, I can finish them by myself. I need you to do something else for me."

His father led him into the very last place he wanted to be—the toolshed. The gargoyle was lying on its back on the worktable, just the way they'd left it the other day. Michael could barely stand to look at the thing, let alone touch it again. But what excuse could he give to his father? A thought struck him.

"Hey, Dad, you know how you said that gargoyle is so valuable and all?" Michael paused. "Well, isn't it dumb to put it back on the roof? What if it falls again? It could get smashed. Then it wouldn't be worth a thing."

"It's not going to fall again," Mr. Buckner assured him.

"Okay." Michael tried again. "But maybe you should think about selling it. You could use the money to fix some other things around this place. Like, the solarium." The solarium was an old porch that no one ever used anymore. When they had first moved into Moonight Mansion, Michael's mom had talked about replacing the old structure with a modern glass one. She had wanted to fill it with plants all year long.

His dad smiled. "I don't think the gargoyle is worth enough to pay for a room like that. But it's a nice idea, Michael." Mr. Buckner looked a little wistful. "I wish you kids liked this place more. It's a terrific house. I know we haven't done much yet to fix it up. But we're making a start now. You know, old houses like this have a lot of character."

Yeah, great, Michael thought to himself. *If you like being scared out of your wits. Sure, that's great character.*

31

There was no avoiding it. He was going to have to face the gargoyle sooner or later. Steeling himself, Michael turned to the worktable. A big square chunk of stone was lying next to the statue. It was the base that had attached the gargoyle to the roof, he realized.

"What's that doing here?" Michael asked.

"That's your job today," his father answered. "I noticed the base got damaged. See the place where it's chipped off? I want you to repair it."

"Me?" Michael stared at his dad. "How?"

"I bought this stone-repair kit," his father said. He showed Michael a can filled with a gray substance. *Stone filler*, Michael read on the label.

"Use a wooden stick to mix the goop with water," Mr. Buckner told him. "Stir it really well in a metal bucket. Then slather it onto the base and build it up. When it dries it'll be as hard as the original stone. After that, you just file it into shape." His father beamed at him. "Good as new. Isn't that great?"

"Yeah, great," Michael mumbled.

"It's pretty simple, Michael. You can do it. Just make sure you follow the directions." Mr. Buckner reached out and patted the stone gargoyle. "Don't worry, old fella. We'll get you fixed up in no time."

Michael shuddered. How could his dad touch the thing that way? As if he actually liked it?

"All right. I'll leave you to it," Mr. Buckner told him. "Yell if you need help."

With a sigh, Michael filled a bucket with water and started to mix in the goop. He glanced at the base to see how much filler he would need.

There was something carved into the stone, he noticed. He moved in for a closer look. Words or letters . . . he could just barely make them out. They were like those symbols on Egyptian tombs—what did you call them? Hieroglyphics.

Michael gulped at the thought. What if the gargoyle came out of some tomb? It would be just like old Jonah Carter to decorate his revolting house with some ancient statue bearing a curse.

Still, it was almost cool, too—a bit like something from one of the old horror movies he liked to watch, starring Arthur Manheim, who Michael thought was one of the greatest horror actors of all time.

Michael bent closer to the base. He wanted to make some sense out of the carvings. That's what Arthur Manheim would have done. The wooden stick he was holding slipped from his hand. *Klutz*, he scolded himself. He stooped down to lift it.

Was that a noise he heard? "Who's—" He stood up sharply. Something smashed against his head. Hard. Then everything went black.

CHAPTER 6

"Michael?"

Michael blinked.

"Michael, are you okay?"

He forced his eyes to focus on the person above him. It was Sara.

"What are you doing down there?" she asked.

"That's a good question," he said. She put out a hand to help him up.

"Wow! That protein drink is working. You are really bulking up," Sara said. "You weigh a ton."

Michael sat upright. He felt a little dizzy and his head was throbbing. He reached up to feel it.

"Ouch!" He winced in pain. "There's a big lump right over my ear."

"Well, don't touch it, dummy!" Gently, Sara pushed his hair aside to get a good look. "Wow." She whistled. "That's pretty nasty. We should get some ice on it. How'd you get it, anyway? Karate chopping the gargoyle?"

"Ha ha. What a comedian. Actually, I was

leaning down to get this stick. Next thing I knew I was on the ground, looking up at you."

"You must have bashed your head on the statue," she said. "Right here, where it's sticking out over the edge of the table."

"Guess so," Michael muttered. "That thing could knock out an elephant."

He forced himself to stand. *Steady, boy*, he told himself. He still felt a little shaky. He grabbed the edge of the table to steady himself.

"Wait a minute, Sara. That statue wasn't sticking over the edge of the table before. I swear it wasn't."

"Come on, Michael. Stone statues that weigh a thousand pounds don't exactly jump around."

"But we're not just talking about any old statue," Michael reminded her. "We're talking about a gargoyle in the House of Horrors."

Sara frowned. "You're serious," she said. "You're really worried about the gargoyle."

"Well, yeah, a little." Michael glanced uneasily at the statue. "Remember what Jonah Carter told us? His ghost, I mean. After it tried to burn us to death?"

"Sure," Sara answered. "He said he'd be back. But I just don't think Jonah Carter's evil spirit is in that gargoyle."

"Why not?"

"Because if it was, he'd do something a lot worse than just knocking you on the head."

That made some sense, Michael had to admit. He frowned. He wished his head didn't hurt so much. He couldn't think straight. There was something else he wanted to tell Sara. Something about the gargoyle. But what was it?

"Anyway, there's something strange going on around here," Michael persisted. "I haven't told you everything."

Sara took a step closer to him. "Like what?"

Michael lowered his voice. "Well, like this morning, my jaw got stuck."

"What do you mean, stuck?"

"I mean, I opened my mouth to yawn and my jaw got stuck. It wouldn't close again. And it happened later, too. In school." Michael could tell Sara wasn't very impressed.

"So, what does that have to do with anything?" Sara asked.

"I'm not sure," Michael said. But he knew there was something wrong. Something that he couldn't put his finger on.

"It's not just my jaw," he continued. "What about my fingernails growing so fast? And I've been feeling really stiff all over lately."

Sara thought a minute. "You know, I think it's all the exercise you're getting. That and the protein drink. How much of that stuff are you swigging anyway? Way too much, I bet." At Michael's guilty look, she nodded. "I thought so.

And everyone gets sore when they're not used to working out. Let's face it, Michael. You just started this karate business. You were never exactly Mr. Fitness."

Michael thought about Mr. Morse, his social studies teacher. One of Mr. Morse's favorite health lectures was on the importance of stretching before and after exercising. Which Michael had to admit, he seldom did. Maybe his sister had a point. But still . . .

"But the gargoyle really *did* hit me on the head," he insisted.

Sara looked doubtful. "I'm not saying it couldn't have happened. With this stupid house, anything is possible. But—"

Michael heard footsteps approaching. "Shhh!" he warned. "It's Dad." They couldn't talk about Jonah Carter or the evil in the *casa del mondo creepioso* around their parents.

Mr. Buckner came into the shed. "How's it going, Michael? Finished with the filler yet?"

Michael had forgotten all about the goop.

"I hope you remembered to empty the bucket when you were finished," his father said. "You can't let it sit around too long. It'll get hard as a rock. You *did* finish, didn't you?"

Michael gave a weak smile. "Well, uh, I *stirred* it really well, Dad. But then I sort of got interrupted, and—"

"Oh, no. Don't tell me." Mr. Buckner glanced at the bucket on the worktable. Then he looked at the base. "Michael—you didn't even start to patch that chip yet." Mr. Buckner groaned. He grabbed hold of the stick, poked it in the bucket of goop, and tried to stir it. The stick snapped off in his hand.

"Sorry, Dad," Michael mumbled.

"Now I'll have to buy another batch of this stuff," his father complained. "And probably a new bucket, too." Mr. Buckner lifted the bucket. "Oof," he grunted. "It's heavy."

"Maybe we can soften the filler somehow," Michael suggested hopefully. "Here, Dad, give the bucket to me."

Mr. Buckner shook his head. "There's no way you could soften this."

Michael tried to take the bucket away from his father.

"No, Michael. It's too heavy for you," Mr. Buckner began. "Here, let me—"

"Really, Dad. I can fix it!" Michael grabbed the bucket with both hands and tugged. Mr. Buckner gave him a look of surprise as the bucket slipped out of his grasp.

Michael threw his arms around the bucket and hugged it against his chest. There was a funny crunching noise. Michael noticed that his father was staring at him with a strange look on his face.

Sara's mouth had dropped open.

"What?" Michael asked. He glanced down at the bucket. *But—that's impossible*, he thought in disbelief. *It can't be!*

CHAPTER 7

Michael let go of the bucket. It slipped from his hands and crashed onto the worktable.

"You crushed it!" Sara stared at the bucket in shock.

One side of the bucket was crumpled up like a ball of aluminum foil. The heavy stone filler that had been rock-hard a few minutes ago was crushed into small gravel-shaped pieces. Some of it spilled out onto the tabletop.

"Michael, that was incredible." Mr. Buckner shook his head in amazement. "That karate is something!" Michael's father lifted the bucket and turned it over and over. "I guess you hit this thing at just the right spot," he said.

Michael ran his tongue over his lips, which were suddenly very dry. "Uh, sure, Dad. Karate," Michael murmured. His eyes met Sara's. Something weird was definitely going on here. Something really weird.

"Well, you know, Dad," Sara jumped in quickly. "Michael's really been working out lately. And that protein drink of his—it really adds weight. Helps you bulk up," she added.

"Yeah. All the guys are, uh, getting really strong," Michael put in.

Mr. Buckner looked impressed. He fingered the crushed bucket again. "Unbelievable," he said. "Well, Michael, I guess we'll have to try fixing that base again tomorrow. In the meantime, take it easy with that karate. You don't seem to know your own strength." He left the toolshed chuckling to himself.

Michael felt his forehead break out in a sweat. "Sara," he said softly. "I hardly touched that bucket. And look at it! I really crushed it! This is . . . This is way too creepy." He could barely get the words out. "There is something really wrong with me."

Sara looked worried. "Yeah. I guess you were right. It is pretty weird that you're so strong all of a sudden."

Michael stared at the gargoyle. "I wish I knew what was going on."

"Let's get out of here," Sara suggested. "This stupid statue is giving us *both* the creeps."

"Good idea," Michael muttered. "I'm going to go upstairs. I have to write three hundred words about jute. And then I'm going to take that protein drink and throw it down the drain." Michael glanced at his hands. His nails had grown past his fingertips. "And file these nails—again," he added.

That night Michael dreamed he was racing through the jungle. Vines whipped at his face. As he came into a clearing, a tiger charged at him. It raked its claws across his face. Michael threw up his arm in a karate punch. The tiger crumbled into pieces.

Michael blinked. Sunlight streamed into his bedroom. He sat up and looked around. Everything was where it should be. His new Michael Jordan poster was taped over his desk. His dinosaur collection—Michael loved dinosaurs—was sprawled over the top of his dresser, as usual. And his boxed set of Arthur Manheim horror movies was on his bookshelf.

Michael stretched, opened his mouth in a wide yawn—and closed it again. Easily. He really was okay! His muscles felt pretty good, too. Not too stiff. He balled his hands up into fists and rubbed his eyes.

Ow! Michael stared at his nails. They were about two inches long. *Not again!* He tried not to feel sick to his stomach.

"Michael! Sara!" their mother called up the stairs. "Breakfast! Hurry or you'll both be late for school!"

"Okay, Mom. I'm coming," Michael yelled back. He grabbed the metal file and went to work on his nails. Then he threw on his clothes and hurried down to the kitchen. His dad watched as he gulped down mouthfuls of juice, milk, and muffins.

"Now that's a decent breakfast," his father said in approval. "That'll keep up your strength!"

"Yeah," Michael mumbled through a mouthful of crumbs. He didn't want to think about his newfound strength. If he kept dwelling on it he'd never be able to get through the day. It was clear that the house was up to its old tricks, but until something else happened he'd try not to worry too much.

His father beamed at him. "That was a great stunt with the bucket yesterday," he said. "I'm proud of you, working so hard at your karate class. I'm glad you're learning the art of self-defense."

I'd rather learn the art of demolishing Tucker Tropowsky, Michael thought. He brightened. Maybe there was a bright side to his strength after all.

He thought about it again later that afternoon in karate class as he stared into Tucker's mean little eyes. Mr. Dooley had just finished leading them through the beginning exercises.

"Okay. Now change partners," Mr. Dooley ordered. "We'll try those kick-punch combinations again. And remember—no contact. This practice is for form only."

Michael was more than happy to move across the mat and face Max. Tucker snorted as he changed places. "See you later, Buckner," he taunted.

Ignoring Tucker, Michael bowed at his best friend, who bowed in return. Then he and Max began to circle each other. Max opened with a kick. Michael tried a kick as well.

"Good form, boys," Mr. Dooley told them before moving on to the next mat.

Michael and Max kept circling each other. Next, Max tried a short, jabbing punch. Michael decided to try the same move. But as he came forward, Max suddenly darted toward him. Michael's left hand scraped against Max's cheek.

"Ow!" Max yelped. "What did you do to me?" He swiped at his cheek. A few drops of blood appeared on his fingers.

"I . . . I guess my nails got a little long," Michael said. He glanced down at his hands and caught his breath.

His nails had grown since the morning. It wasn't possible. He had filed them down to the tips of his fingers. Now they were over an inch long.

Nails don't grow that fast, Michael thought wildly. *Not on normal people.*

What was going on?

CHAPTER 8

Michael tried not to show how upset he was.

"What's wrong?" Max asked him.

"Not now," Michael kept his voice low. "I'll tell you after class."

"Yeah, but—you should do something about those nails," Max complained. "They hurt!"

"What's that about Buckner's nails?" Tucker left his mat and leaned over to get a glimpse. He pushed up next to Michael to get a glimpse. "Hey! Get a load of those hands! What'd you do, Buckner? Have 'em done in the beauty shop?"

"Shut up," Max told Tucker.

"You don't need *karate* for self-defense," Tucker cried. "You've got long nails!"

It was the last straw. Michael charged at Tucker, grabbed one of his arms, and pulled— hard. Tucker flipped cleanly over Michael's back and landed on the mat with a loud thud. He sprawled there with a look of shock on his face.

If Michael hadn't been shocked himself, he would have laughed. Mr. Dooley hurried over to them. "Get back, now. Give him air." The teacher knelt down on the mat. "Tucker. Are you all right?"

Tucker nodded and struggled to his feet.

"On this mat, then, both of you," Mr. Dooley ordered.

He looked very angry. "Not a bad flip, Michael," he snapped. "Remind me to show you the right way to do it—another time. But not now. Now, you show Tucker some respect."

Mr. Dooley placed Michael and Tucker opposite each other on the mat.

"Michael, you bow to Tucker," Mr. Dooley said. "Tucker, you bow to Michael."

For the next half an hour, Michael and Tucker had to stand there and pretend they liked each other. Mr. Dooley made the whole class listen while he went on and on about discipline and respect and learning to follow instructions.

Finally, Mr. Dooley dismissed the class. Michael had no desire to listen to any more of the teacher's talk. But there was something he had to know.

"Uh, Mr. Dooley," Michael began. He lowered his voice. "Listen, is it normal to get stiff after karate practice? I mean, really stiff. So stiff you feel like you weigh a thousand pounds, and your muscles keep getting, uh, stuck?"

Mr. Dooley cracked a smile. "You take a long soak in epsom salts and you'll be fine," he told Michael. He clapped Michael on the back and frowned.

"You *are* stiff," he said. "Your muscles are as hard as a rock. You do what I said—take a long hot soak tonight. And learn to relax!"

Michael hurried out of the gym with Max at his side.

"Boy, you sure nailed Tropowsky with that flip." Max grinned. "It was great!"

"Yeah, I guess so." Michael stared at his nails again. "Listen, Max, about these nails—"

"Yeah." Max tapped his cheek. The scratch had dried into a long, thin scab. "You've gotta cut those things."

"I know. I know. Max, have you been taking your protein drink?"

"Sure. Not that it's doing anything. I haven't gained an ounce."

"Well, it's done something to me," Michael said. "I think maybe the drink made my nails grow like this. Only—" He paused. "Only, why didn't it make your nails grow?"

Max shrugged. "I don't know. We're different. So what?"

"So, have you been getting really stiff and sore after practice?" Michael asked.

"Sometimes," Max answered. "I just stretch and soak in the tub a few minutes."

"That's what Mr. Dooley told me to do," Michael said thoughtfully. He was quiet a moment. "Listen, Max, do you think it's strange how strong I am all of a sudden? I mean, you're taking the same class and none of this stuff is happening to you."

"Maybe you work out harder. I've kind of blown off my weight lifting," Max admitted.

It wasn't weight lifting, Michael knew. "Feel my muscles," he told Max.

Max reached out and pressed Michael's arm. "Wow," he said. "You are solid. You've been lifting extra weights or something, right?"

"No," Michael told him. "But I keep getting stronger anyway. Remember how I broke that board? Well, last night, I crushed a metal bucket. And then today, when I flipped Tropowsky across the room—" Michael paused. "He didn't weigh anything, Max. It was like . . . like flipping a feather."

Max stared at him. "Well, it's supposed to be that way. That's what karate is all about, right? Size doesn't count."

"I'm not that good at karate," Michael pointed out. He swallowed hard. "The thing is, what if karate and protein drinks aren't doing this to me? What if it's something else?"

"Like what?" Max asked.

"I don't know," Michael answered. "I just don't know!"

48

That evening, he had a hard time getting through dinner. Mostly, he felt sick to his stomach.

"You're not eating much, Michael," his mother finally said. "Do you feel okay?"

"Sure, Mom." To prove it, Michael grabbed a big chunk of bread and started to lift it to his mouth. His arm got about as high as the table top before it felt so stiff that he couldn't move it anymore. He looked at Sara, panicked.

"Well?" his mother asked. "What are you waiting for?"

"Nothing," Michael mumbled. "Um, my arm is kind of stiff, that's all."

"Must be a muscle spasm," Sara put in hastily.

"Must be," their dad agreed. "From all that karate practice. Are you stretching enough, Michael?"

"Yeah, plenty," he said distractedly. His mother was staring at his outstretched arm. *Oh, no!* he realized. *My nails!*

His nails had grown at least another half inch since karate class. Quickly, he raised his other arm and forced the stiff arm into his lap. But his mother had seen his hands.

"Michael! Those nails!" she cried in dismay. "They're disgusting."

"May I be excused, then?" Michael asked. "I'll go take care of them." He got up to leave the

49

table, but he felt so stiff and slow he could hardly push his chair back.

He dragged himself up to his room and plunked down on the edge of his bed. He had never felt so tired before. *I've got to take one of those epsom salt baths tonight*, he told himself. *That would take care of the stiffness*. He hoped.

Sara barged into his room without bothering to knock. "Listen, Michael, I—" she gasped and stared at her brother with a look of horror on her face.

"What?" His throat felt tight and stiff, too, he noticed. He swallowed and raised a hand to scratch a sudden itch he felt behind his ear. Sara's eyes grew even wider.

"Michael—" Her voice was a whisper. "Your hand. It's all curled up like . . . like a claw!" She hesitated. "And your nails. Don't they look like . . . like talons?"

Michael shook his head slowly. It almost hurt to move his neck. "No," he protested. "Not talons." He tried to hide his hands behind his back.

Sara stared at him. "And your face—"

She stopped talking. Michael saw the fear in her eyes.

"My face? There's nothing wrong with my face!" Sara kept staring at him.

"Stop looking at me like that!" he cried.

"Oh, Michael . . ." Sara ran to the dresser and

came back with a hand mirror. She held it up to his face. "Look at yourself."

Michael had to bite his tongue to keep from screaming. He felt sick to his stomach again—really sick, this time.

He hardly recognized his face. There were deep lines going from his nose to his mouth. Lines that had never been there before. His eyes were sunken deep into their sockets. And his lips were stretched out in a thin line, so that his whole mouth was twisted into a grotesque scowl.

Michael tore his eyes away from the mirror.

"You see it. Don't you?" Sara whispered.

Michael nodded. He forced himself to look at his face again. He looked like . . . he looked just like . . .

Michael wanted to throw down the mirror.

He looked just like the gargoyle!

CHAPTER 9

Michael dropped his head into his hands and moaned. "No! This can't be happening! I'm turning into a . . . a monster." He shuddered at the thought.

Sara gazed back at him with a helpless look on her face. "I'm sorry, Michael."

Sorry! Michael felt like tearing the house down, piece by piece—smashing it just like he'd smashed the tiger in his dream. This was definitely the worst thing that had happened to him in the House of Horrors.

This was worse than anything. Because it was happening *inside* him—to his own body.

"It's the evil," Michael whispered to Sara. "The evil is back."

Sara nodded. "But I don't get it. This is so different from the other things that happened."

"I know," Michael said. "Grown-ups never saw the evil stuff before. But Mr. Morse saw my jaw get stuck. And Mr. Dooley said my muscles were hard as rocks. And Mom and Dad both saw my fingernails."

Michael felt a burst of fear. "We've got to do something!" he cried out.

"Okay, now," Sara said, trying to calm him down. "Take it easy. This is no time to panic. We have to think."

"I've already done that!" Michael said. "I've been thinking about it, nonstop. So what? That doesn't help one bit."

"Well, did something like this ever happen in one of your Arthur Manheim movies?" Sara asked.

"No," Michael said. "I mean, he played a mad scientist who turns invisible in *Doctor Fearsome Returns*. But that's not a thing like what's happening to me."

Sara frowned. "Didn't he do a movie about a stone statue in Egypt?"

"That was about a mummy!" Michael nearly screamed. He was starting to feel a little desperate. They had to *do* something. They couldn't sit there talking about Arthur Manheim movies— no matter how much Michael liked them.

"You're way off," he snapped at Sara. "That mummy movie was about some archaeologist digging in an old tomb and he discovers some hierog—"

Michael sat up taller on the bed.

"What? Discovers what?" Sara asked.

"Hieroglyphics!" Michael nearly shouted. He felt a wave of relief. And excitement. "You know, those pictures that Egyptians used instead of writing! Hieroglyphics! That's what I was trying to remember!" His stiff mouth stretched into something that was almost a smile.

Sara stared at him as if he were crazy.

"The statue base!" Michael explained. "Yesterday, when I was in the toolshed. I saw these weird hieroglyphics or something, carved into the statue's base. I was trying to figure them out. That's when the gargoyle knocked me over the head!"

"Listen, Michael," Sara said patiently. "I know you're really upset and everything—but what are you talking about?"

"Don't you get it? I saw the writing on the base. Then the gargoyle knocked me out. I think it wanted to stop me from looking at them."

Now Sara looked excited, too. "Then we'd better go take another look at that base," she said.

"Yes!" Michael cheered. He got up as fast as he could, which wasn't very fast.

Outside his room, the hallway was quiet. Their parents were still downstairs, watching television. Michael and Sara crept down the stairs and out through the kitchen. Michael paused at the door to the backyard. It was raining outside.

Michael's hands were curled up too tightly to

do much, so after Sara threw on her jacket, she helped Michael with his. She grabbed the flashlight.

They crossed the yard without saying anything. Sara glanced up at the roof of the house. "Well, there's one good thing that's happened," she said, breaking the silence.

"What's that?"

"Well, Dad got the roof fixed before this rainstorm," she joked weakly.

Michael tried to roll his eyes, but gave up the effort.

Once they were inside the shed, Sara turned on the flashlight and aimed it at the gargoyle. They both stared at it for a moment. It was lying on the worktable just as they'd left it, with its blank eyes staring up at the ceiling.

Or were they? Michael could have sworn those creepy empty eyes had glanced at them—at him—as they'd come in.

He felt a cold chill go down his spine. Behind him, Sara nudged his arm.

"Come on," she whispered.

They walked over to the base and Sara shone the flashlight onto the stone. They could see half-letters and broken lines. Nothing that made any kind of sense.

Sara looked thoughtful. "You know, we did an art project in school once. You take some paper and you put it over a carving and rub over it with a pencil. The pencil fills in the broken spaces and you can see the whole carving better."

"Maybe you should try it," Michael suggested. *He* had no intention of touching the thing, not if he could help it.

Sara found some scrap paper and a pencil and went to work. A few minutes later she shone the flashlight onto the rubbing.

"That looks like half an 'S,'" she said, connecting the lines.

"And that's probably an 'N,'" Michael pointed out.

Sara worked quickly on the rest of the rubbing. A few minutes later she was finished. They both stared down at the message.

Impulsively, Michael grabbed the paper, crumpled it, and threw it into a trash can. But he couldn't forget what he'd seen. The words would not go away.

"Flesh becomes stone," he whispered. "Stone becomes flesh."

CHAPTER 10

Michael shuddered. "Let's get out of here!" he cried. He and Sara bolted from the toolshed. They slogged back through the wet yard into the kitchen again.

Sara had to help Michael peel off his wet jacket. He collapsed onto a kitchen chair and sat with his head in his hands.

"Don't worry, Michael. We'll think of something." She reached out to pat his arm. "Yikes!" she cried.

"Now what?"

"Your arm—" Sara jabbed a finger into his bare skin. "It's so rough. I mean, seriously rough—like an alligator or something."

"Gee, I guess I'll have to use some skin cream on it," Michael said, trying to make a joke. "Do you have some? Or should I borrow it from Mom? Or maybe one of the girls at school—" Michael felt his voice rising higher and higher. He was getting hysterical.

57

I'm really losing it, he thought.

"It's okay," Sara assured him. "Look, Michael, I just thought of something. The stiffness only gets really bad at night, doesn't it?

Michael tried to think. "Maybe. So far it seems to be worse at night. Except for my jaw being stiff—that can happen anytime, I think. And these nails—" Michael held them up and stared at them. They had grown again. "These nails grow all the time."

"Well, keep filing," Sara told him. "The important thing is, most of the gargoyle stuff gets better in the morning."

For a moment, both Sara and Michael were silent. Michael guessed that they were both thinking the same thing. At some point, the stiffness *wasn't* going to get better in the morning. It wasn't going to get better at all. Ever.

"Don't worry," Sara said. Michael could tell she was trying to sound confident. "Whatever is happening, it's happening slowly. We've got some time to figure this out."

"But, how much time?"

Sara ignored that. "We can stop it, Michael. I know we can. We've stopped the evil so far. Haven't we? And—" She broke off.

The swinging door to the kitchen suddenly flew open. Mr. Buckner appeared, balancing two plates and glasses in his arms. He stopped when he saw Michael and Sara at the table.

"What are you two doing here? I thought you went to bed ages ago."

"Uh, we did," Sara answered. "We were, um, looking for a snack."

Mr. Buckner gave them both a curious look. Michael quickly ducked to keep his father from seeing his face. He dropped his hands into his lap, too.

But Mr. Buckner wasn't looking at Michael. He yawned as he set the dirty dishes in the sink. "Well, your mother and I are turning in," he told them. "You'd better do the same or you'll never get up in time for school."

"We know, Dad. We're going up in a minute," Sara said.

As soon as their father was gone, Sara shook Michael's shoulder. "Research, Michael! That's what we haven't done."

"Huh?" he said.

"Research," Sara repeated. "We've got to learn more about what's happening to you. Like, who put those words on the statue base? Some old sculptor? Or Jonah Carter himself? We need to find out."

"Yeah, like I'd feel tons better knowing that," Michael retorted. "And just where are you going to find this information?"

Sara was silent.

"I knew it! Listen, Sara, I am not going into that creepy old den to look for some creepy old book again."

Michael noticed that Sara didn't look so eager about that, either. When the ghost of Jonah Carter had appeared, it had made Sara search through all the books in the den to find a special poem, and Michael had helped her. Neither of them would ever forget what happened there. Sara's wrist nearly got smashed in a secret panel. And then the whole wall of bookshelves had almost crushed them.

"We searched through every one of those books," he reminded Sara now. "Did you see anything about gargoyles?"

"No," she admitted. "And there's nothing about gargoyles in the poems that Jonah Carter wrote, either. I should know. I've read them all about a million times."

"Okay. Then we don't have to go through that again."

"But we never searched the attic for books," Sara pointed out.

Michael stared at her in disbelief. The attic! It was one of the creepiest places in the House of Horrors—much creepier than the den. It was always freezing cold, and dark, and full of spider webs. If there was one thing Michael hated more than anything, it was spiders. He shuddered just thinking about them.

Besides, the last time Sara went up to the attic, the walls had closed in on her and she'd practically been squeezed to death. Not to mention the fact that she'd been attacked by a monster snake. Neither one of those things made Michael want to rush up there to find some book—a book that might not even exist.

"There are whole boxes of books and papers up there," Sara argued. "If there's anything about gargoyles in this house, I bet it's in the attic."

What choice did he have? They needed more information. Sara was right about that. Michael took a deep breath. "Okay. But we can't search tonight." He held up his clawlike hands. "I can't flip through the pages of a book right now."

"All right," Sara said. "I'm not so keen on going up there tonight, anyway. Let's do it tomorrow. Maybe you won't be so stiff in the morning."

Michael nodded. "We'll get up really early. Let's go to bed now. I'm tired."

Early the next morning, Michael dragged himself out of bed. He was sleepy, but he wasn't too stiff, he noticed thankfully. He dressed quickly and met Sara in the hall. The two of them sneaked up to the third floor.

As usual, a blast of icy cold air hit them as soon as they reached the landing. They both paused at the door that led up to the attic. Would the house do something to them? Usually, the house fought back when they tried to stop the evil.

"I'll do this," Michael told Sara. "I'm stronger."

He reached out and grabbed the knob. He gritted his teeth and prepared for the worst. The door might wrap around him.

Or the ceiling might drop down on his head.

The stairs might open beneath him or try to throw him down.

Michael held his breath, turned the knob, and pushed.

CHAPTER 11

The door swung open easily.

Nothing bad had happened!

"This is too weird," Michael said. "Why isn't the house trying to stop us?"

"I don't know," Sara said.

"Maybe it's putting all its powers into the gargoyle," Michael muttered. "Maybe what it's doing to me is so terrible that it needs all of its strength." He couldn't look at Sara when he said it.

"It doesn't matter." Sara patted his shoulder as she followed him up the stairway. "We won't let the house win."

At the top of the stairs, Michael glanced around the attic and shivered. Creepy as always. The morning light made things slightly better. The attic wasn't as creepy as it was at night—but that wasn't saying much.

Sara pointed at a huge old trunk that sat in a

corner. "I remember seeing old papers and note-books in there. I'll start with this."

Michael nodded. "I'll go through these boxes." He squatted next to a pile of old cartons and began to dig through to the bottom. He found plenty of old books and notebooks. But none of them had anything to do with gargoyles. "Nothing," he called to Sara.

"Nothing in here, either," Sara said in frustration.

"Wait a minute. What's this?" Michael pulled out a book with a crumpled cover. "It looks like some kind of science stuff."

He flipped through the pages. One page was completely filled with pictures of the phases of the moon. Michael felt a chill. "This is all about stars and planets," he told Sara. They both knew that Jonah Carter had studied the planets. He had even carved the phases of the moon into the fireplace mantle in their living room.

Michael turned page after page. There was nothing there about gargoyles, though. He threw the book down.

He pulled out the drawers of an old bureau and searched through them. Nothing. He dug through some more cartons. He even plowed through hatboxes and two piles of old table-cloths. Meantime, Sara had been just as thorough in her search. They looked through every trunk and carton in the attic. They hadn't found one bit of information about gargoyles.

"Now what?" Michael frowned.

"Let's go back to the den," Sara said. "We'll have to try the bookshelves again."

"No. There's got be something up here. I have this feeling about it," Michael insisted.

"What choice do we have? Come on, Michael. Let's go *now*. We don't have much time left. Mom and Dad will be awake soon."

Michael still didn't move. He gazed around the attic. They were missing some obvious clue. He knew they were.

Sara pulled at his arm. "Wake up, Michael! We've searched everywhere up here. Everywhere that makes sense."

"That's exactly it, Sara!" Michael's eyes lit up. "So now, let's search where it *doesn't* make sense."

Sara looked at him for an instant. "You're right. That's just what Jonah Carter would do. Hide the information someplace we'd never dream of searching. But where?"

Michael scanned the attic again. What *hadn't* they searched yet? "How about that trunk full of costumes?"

"Nope. I checked it already."

"And I looked through the boxes of shoes. Even the crate full of old pots and pans." Michael frowned. So where *hadn't* they looked?

His eyes swept past the enormous stuffed

bear that stood in one corner. He stared at the windowsills, and the dark, shadowy place between the roof and the old wooden pillars, and the—

He jerked his head back again. "The bear!"

He ran across the attic and stood in front of the huge stuffed animal. He and Sara had always avoided it. For one thing, it was gigantic—standing on its hind legs it was almost twice as tall as he was. And it looked disgusting. Its black fur was old and ratty and caked with years of dust.

Not to mention the bear's expression. It looked angry—really angry. Michael shuddered as he stared into its tiny yellow eyes. *The eyes of a killer*, he thought. Which made it the perfect guardian.

"Sara!" Michael cried. "I bet old Jonah hid his gargoyle stuff somewhere near that bear. We never go near it, right? And it's the one thing in this attic that we've never even touched."

He ran over to it and began patting it all over.

Sara hurried to his side.

"Maybe he stuffed a book inside this thing," Michael said. "Or maybe—"

Suddenly he stopped. One of the floorboards around the bear was very squeaky, he realized. It was loose. He leaned over and tried to pry the board up. It refused to budge.

"Be careful," Sara warned.

Michael grunted. Using all his strength, he pulled at the board. It held tight. Michael kept at it. "Come on, you—"

With a crack, the old board gave way. Michael threw it aside and peered into the space it had left.

"Nothing!" he cried in dismay. "It's empty."

He stared at Sara. "I don't get it. I felt sure there was something under there—"

"What's that noise?" Sara interrupted.

Michael glanced around. The wide board had run under one of the sturdy wooden pillars that held up the attic roof. Michael's stomach dropped. "The pillar . . ." he whispered.

The thick wooden pillar swayed back and forth. A cloud of dust puffed out as the pillar began to topple.

Sara was standing right in its path.

"Sara!" Michael yelled. "Move!"

But Sara was frozen in place, a look of terror in her eyes. Michael jumped up, knocking the bear over in his haste.

Michael ran toward his sister.

What could he do? There wasn't time. No time.

He squeezed his eyes shut and threw himself against the pillar.

CHAPTER 12

The pillar crashed down, right into him. He wrapped his arms around it and pushed. His knees buckled. For a moment, he thought he would fall. But he held on, and something happened as he did.

Sara threw a frightened glance at the ceiling. "How long can you hold that?" she cried. "The ceiling will collapse and crush us, Michael!"

A grin slowly spread across his face. "I think I could hold this forever. It's as light as a feather!"

Michael chuckled. Then he hoisted the pillar over his head and shoved it back under the roof. It slid easily into place. The roof seemed to groan, but the pillar held.

Sara gaped at Michael. "That was incredible," she finally managed to say.

"Hey, being as strong as a gargoyle comes in handy sometimes." Michael shrugged. He turned to Sara. "Are you all—" he stopped, his gaze locked onto the floor.

"Sara—look!" He pointed at the spot where the bear had been. Now that it had been pushed aside, they could see a metal handle attached to the floor. Michael and Sara knelt beside it and Michael grasped the handle.

"Don't pull too hard," Sara warned. "Or this time, you might rip up the whole attic!"

Michael tugged on the handle very gently. "Hey, it's attached to a trapdoor," he cried. The small door swung open. Underneath it there was a square space. In the space was a book. It was covered with a thick layer of dust.

"Yes!" Michael cheered. He leaned over and stared into the hiding place. Michael swallowed. Another book. Jonah seemed to have a thing about books. Would this one be as creepy as the one they'd found before?

"What are you waiting for?" Sara asked.

Michael looked up at her. "I kind of don't want to touch it," he admitted. "It sort of gives me the creeps."

"I know. But nothing bad happened when I touched that book of Jonah's poems," Sara reminded him. "The *book* can't hurt us, Michael."

"Yeah," he said. "But what's *in* it can."

"Give it to me then," Sara ordered. She held out her hand. Michael noticed that she didn't reach into the hiding place herself.

"I'll do it." He grabbed the book. It felt perfectly normal. He blew onto the cover. A thick cloud of dust swirled into his face. Michael coughed. "Yuck!" He gasped. "Remind me not to do *that* again."

Where the dust had cleared he could see gold writing on the book's cracked leather cover.

"Wow," he said softly.

"What?" Sara cried. "What does it say?"

"The Journal of Jonah Carter," Michael read. He whistled. "This is Jonah Carter's own diary!"

Michael opened the cover. Sara leaned over his shoulder.

"That's the same handwriting we saw in the book of poems," she cried.

Michael squinted. Jonah's spidery handwriting was pretty hard to make out. The old brown ink was faded and in some places it disappeared completely. Michael started flipping through the pages.

"There's a whole section on gargoyles!" Michael told her. He scanned the pages quickly. "It says here that people believed that gargoyles could ward off evil spirits. But the gargoyles themselves weren't evil." Michael turned over a few more pages.

"Wow! He's written the whole history of Moonlight Mansion in here," Michael murmured. He cleared his throat. "Listen to this."

Moonlight Mansion. The perfect name
for this perfect gift to my beloved wife.

*A house for her. A house that shim-
mers with the magic of moonlight, as
she shimmers—with all the pale
beauty of the moon.*

"Sounds like more poetry," Sara said.
"Yeah, but the important thing is, he built this
place as a present for his wife," Michael told her.
"And look here—I think his wife died."
Michael read another passage to Sara:

*How will I live without her? Save for
our precious babe, I would join her, as
she walks among the angels!*

Michael frowned in confusion. "What exactly
does that mean?" he asked.
"It means that Elizabeth Carter was born!"
Sara cried.
"He sure was crazy about his daughter,"
Michael commented. He showed Sara another
diary entry:

*Elizabeth grows dearer to me each
day. She is the joy of my heart—the
sweetest treasure I have.*

"Then what happens?" Sara asked.
"Nothing special," Michael told her as he
flipped through more pages. "Hold on—what's

this?" Michael bent closer over the book.

"What? Let me see," Sara said, trying to push him aside.

"Looks like big trouble," Michael said. "I think Elizabeth was really sick or something." He pointed where he was reading:

> *Doctor Palmer here again today. Not much hope is left. I have done as the doctor asked. I have hidden her from the sunlight that causes my dear one so much pain. Her little dark chamber holds my only hope. My poor child. Do not leave me, Elizabeth!*

"It's about the secret room!" Sara gasped. "Now we know why it's so dark in there. Sunshine hurt Elizabeth."

Michael and Sara already knew that the hidden room had belonged to Elizabeth Carter. They had found her drawings there, and a silver hairbrush with the initials E.C. carved on the back.

Michael turned more pages of the diary. Jonah's handwriting became even wilder and harder to read. For several pages the scribbles made no sense at all. There weren't even any complete sentences. Only snatches of phrases: "Beauty eternal!" and "Life evermore!"

"What's he getting at?" Michael wondered.

"I don't know yet," Sara said. "But then, look at this page, Michael! His writing has changed again."

They bent over the diary together. The next entries were written in a very small, very tight handwriting, as if Jonah had put a lot of effort into each word. The pages were incredibly neat. But they weren't like a diary at all. They looked more like long lists.

"These look like recipes," Sara remarked, turning the pages.

"No, they look like experiments!" Michael grabbed the book from Sara's hands. "They are—reports of scientific experiments that Jonah tried." Michael's cheeks turned pale. He turned to Sara with a look of horror on his face. "Did you see this?" he asked.

> *My experiments continue. They say I should leave this house. But I will not walk in the sunlight. Until I bring her back, no child shall draw breath in this house! Only her! I will make her live again!*

Sara gaped at Michael in astonishment. "That's why he hates us," she cried. "That's why he swore he'd never let us live! Jonah Carter doesn't want any children to live in *her* house!"

"Yeah, but he was a lousy scientist," Michael

said angrily. "He created a lot of evil. And now the evil is out to get me!"

"We can stop him," Sara said weakly.

"Oh, yeah?" Michael asked. "How?" He picked up the diary again. "Look at this."

> *Whom the gargoyle wounds will a gargoyle become.*
> *Flesh becomes stone. Stone becomes flesh.*

"He's trying to take *my* life, Sara," Michael exclaimed. "The gargoyle wounded *me*. He scratched my arm the day he fell off the base. And that's when I started changing." He stared at his sister.

Suddenly he drew in a deep breath through clenched teeth. "He won't get away with it!" He jumped up and sprang toward the attic door.

Sara's eyes widened in alarm. "Michael, where are you going?"

"To stop that gargoyle!" he shouted. He raced down the attic steps. His legs felt stiffer now, but he was too angry to let it stop him.

He flew down the three flights of stairs and out through the kitchen door. Sara had to scramble to keep up with him. Michael ran across the lawn and into the toolshed.

The cool white stone of the gargoyle shone in the half-darkness.

"I'm as hard as stone, too! I can smash you!" Michael yelled. "I'll crush you like I crushed the stone in that bucket! I'll crush you to bits!"

With all his might Michael delivered the best karate punch of his life—right to the gargoyle's neck.

CHAPTER 13

His hand connected. It sank briefly into the statue's surface. And stayed there. Michael sprang back in horror.

"What—?" He stared at the gargoyle in dismay.

It wasn't crushed. It wasn't even dented.

Michael examined his hand. It wasn't sore or bruised at all. He took a couple of deep breaths to calm himself down. Then he forced himself to reach toward the gargoyle's neck again. His hand trembled as he touched the statue.

The surface was warm. It sank slightly under Michael's fingers as he pressed into it.

"What's happened?" Sara whispered behind him.

"Skin," Michael whispered back. "It feels like skin."

The cool, hard feel of the stone was completely gone. The gargoyle felt rubbery and soft.

Flesh to stone. Stone to flesh.

"This is it." Michael could barely get the words out. His throat was so tight it hurt to speak. "I'm becoming stone. And it's becoming human!"

Sara looked sick.

"We've got to do something," Michael cried. "We have to stop it!" He whirled around wildly. He spotted a huge, jagged-toothed saw hanging on a wall. He grabbed it and raised the sharp blade high above the gargoyle's head.

"Michael! Don't!" Sara screamed.

"Why not?" he yelled back. "It's not stone anymore! I can't crush it now, no matter how strong I am. But maybe I can slice it! Maybe I can slash right through his skin. Maybe he even bleeds."

Sara leaped up at him and hung onto his arm. "No! You can't do anything!" she cried. "Don't you get it?"

"Get what?" Michael asked. But he lowered the saw.

Sara swallowed. "You're connected somehow, Michael. You can't hurt it now."

"Why not?" Michael stared back at his sister.

"If you destroy it, we might never be able to get you back again. You could be stuck this way forever—half boy, half statue," Sara warned. "You can't destroy it. Not until we know how to make you human again. We're stuck."

Michael slid down onto the floor of the shed. "What'll we do now?"

"I don't know," Sara told him.

"I'm scared, Sara," Michael whispered. "I'm scared that, this time, Jonah Carter is going to win."

Sara watched him gravely. "I'm scared, too."

Mr. Dooley paced from one end of the gym to the other, barking out a series of commands. The class was supposed to perform the moves as he called them out. But Michael couldn't pay attention to the teacher. All day, his mind had been numb. He tried to stop thinking about the gargoyle, but he couldn't. It didn't help to go over and over what was happening to him. But he couldn't seem to stop.

"Come on, Buckner," he heard Tucker call across the mat. "That was supposed to be a kick, not a punch. Wake up, jerkface."

Mr. Dooley had turned toward the opposite side of the room.

Tucker raised his hand. It was out flat, open and empty.

"Empty hands—empty mind," he taunted. "Remember, Buckner?"

Michael flicked his hand toward Tucker's shoulder. It was only a gentle slap.

But it sent Tucker sprawling across the mat. "Ow!" he yelped. "You little—!"

With a roar, he leaped up and charged at

Michael. Michael saw his fist flying toward his stomach.

Michael didn't move an inch. Tucker's fist slammed into him. Michael felt something soft, almost as if Tucker had tickled his belly.

Tucker let out a howl of pain.

"Are you crazy?" he bellowed. "What'd you do to me?" He cradled his fist in his other hand. "What'd you stick under your shirt? A rock?" Tucker ran to Mr. Dooley and showed the teacher his swollen fingers. Mr. Dooley told Tucker to hold the hand under cold water for a while.

Max snickered gleefully and elbowed Michael. "Way to go!" he cheered. "He deserved that one."

"Yeah," Michael agreed glumly.

"What's the matter?" Max asked. "Tropowsky's an animal. Who cares what happens to him? You are a karate master!"

"Tucker might be an animal, but I'm no master." Michael took a deep breath. "I'm turning into a monster."

"Huh?" Max looked confused.

"Punch me," Michael ordered him. "Go ahead."

Max hesitated. Then he jabbed his own fist at Michael's stomach. "Wow," Max said, impressed. "How *did* you do that?"

"I didn't, Max." Michael lowered his voice. "My house did. Remember how I told you I'm supposed to fix the gargoyle statue?"

Max nodded.

"Well, the gargoyle is after me, Max. The gargoyle is becoming human. And I'm turning into a stone monster."

Max didn't say anything for a minute. Then he threw an arm around Michael's shoulders. "Hey, you'll be okay. I know you. You and Sara have beat that stupid house every time. Why should this time be different?"

"I don't know why," Michael said softly. "But promise me something, Max. In case the house wins—"

"What?" Max asked.

"Promise me *you* won't fight Tropowsky in the karate match." Michael gave Max a weak smile. "He'll pulverize you."

Sara met Michael after karate class and the two of them walked home together. When they reached Moonlight Mansion, they saw two new ladders leaning up against the front of the house. And some kind of huge pulley hung down from the roof. It was attached to a heavy beam by a thick rope. Their father was standing beneath it with his hands on his hips. His eyes were scanning the driveway as if he'd been waiting for them.

"What's going on, Dad?" Michael called. His head started pounding as he hurried up the drive. *Great. All I need now is a crummy headache*, he thought.

"What's all that stuff?" Sara asked as they reached their father.

"I went to the hardware store, remember?" Mr. Buckner gazed directly at Michael. "To get more stone filler to fix the base."

The base? Michael had forgotten all about it. He hadn't exactly been worried about house repairs since his last encounter with the gargoyle. He raised a hand to rub his forehead. His headache was getting worse. He really didn't want any lectures right now.

Mr. Buckner raised an eyebrow. "It's okay, Michael. I took care of a lot of chores today. I fixed the chip in the base myself. Got more stone filler this morning, when I rented this equipment."

Mr. Buckner gestured at the pulley and the ladders behind him. "I thought you could help me get that base installed. Then a couple of the guys at the hardware store said they'd come to check it out before we try to get the gargoyle back up there."

Michael and Sara exchanged uneasy glances. Would their dad notice a change in the gargoyle? They followed him into the toolshed. Mr. Buckner approached the base. He leaned down to check on the stone filler.

"Hmmnh," he said approvingly. "Looks pretty good. This filler is terrific."

Their father gave the gargoyle's back a pat. "Pretty soon we'll be putting this young man back where he came from."

"Don't call him that!" Michael blurted out.

Mr. Buckner looked at Michael in surprise. "What's the matter?" he asked.

"Nothing," Michael muttered.

Mr. Buckner shrugged. "Okay, then. Give me a hand lifting the base, will you?"

Michael hesitated. He didn't want to even touch the base.

"What's the matter, Michael?" his father asked.

"Nothing." Michael reached toward his side of the stone base. His father grabbed hold of the other side.

"Whew," Mr. Buckner whistled. "Is this getting heavier or am I getting older?" He struggled and managed to lift it a couple of inches. Michael still hadn't touched the stone.

"Michael?" his father said sharply. "Are you helping or not?"

"Yeah, okay, Dad," Michael murmured. "I'm helping."

Michael's fingers curled under the hard stone. It gave him a shock. The stone base felt warm. Michael drew his hands back as if he'd burned them. He glanced at his father and rubbed his palms together. "Feels a little warm," he murmured.

His dad rolled his eyes. "What a joker." He grinned.

Michael tried to grin back. But he couldn't.

The stone felt warm to him now—because his own hands were getting colder. As cold as ice.

CHAPTER 14

Together, they lifted the base.

"Sara," Mr. Buckner commanded, "hold that door open for us, will you."

Sara made sure that the shed door was open wide. Michael and his dad carried the base out to the front of the house. Mr. Buckner attached the heavy piece of stone to the end of the heavy rope that hung from the pulley.

"Okay, Michael, you climb the ladder," his dad ordered. "I'll hoist up the base. Sara, you can keep an eye out. Tell us if we're heading in the right direction."

Michael placed a foot on the ladder's lowest rung. The aluminum creaked. He glanced down and saw that the rung was bowed in the middle. He was too heavy! Another step or two and he would crush the ladder.

"Uh, Dad, maybe we should switch places," Michael quickly suggested. "I, uh—I want you to see how strong I am. Please?"

"I don't know," Mr. Buckner began to say.

"I'll show you." Michael hurried over to the pulley. He grasped the end of the rope and gave it a gentle tug. The stone base flew smoothly up on the other end of the rope. It hung about ten feet in the air—almost up to the roof. "And it feels like it doesn't weigh anything," Michael called to his dad.

"You convinced me," Mr. Buckner said. He scurried up the ladder, guiding the base as Michael raised it the rest of the way.

When the base had reached the top of the third-floor gable, Mr. Buckner shoved it hard. It slipped into the empty spot just under the peaked roof.

"Okay, now, I'm setting the bolts," he called down to Michael. He pulled some long metal bolts from his pocket. They passed from the stone base into special steel reinforcement rods that held it to the roof beams. Mr. Buckner grabbed a heavy wrench from his tool belt. He tightened the bolts and gave the wrench an extra twist.

"Okay. That should hold for another two hundred years!" Mr. Buckner climbed down the ladder. "Thanks for helping," he said, throwing an arm around Michael's shoulder. "Whoa. Putting on some serious muscle mass there! This karate is really good for you, huh?"

"Yeah," Michael replied. "It's great."

Mr. Buckner started whistling as he fetched a can of paint. "I'm going to touch up these metal gutters," he said, pointing up to the roof. "Bring me some extra brushes from the shed, okay?"

"Okay, Dad." Michael headed towards the tool-shed. Sara followed after him.

"Don't worry, Michael," she started to say. "I don't think Dad's ready to put the gargoyle back just yet and—"

"I'm sick of hearing about the gargoyle!" Michael snapped.

"Whoa! What'd I do?" Sara stared at him in surprise.

"Sorry. I have a headache, okay?" Michael grumbled. His head was pounding so hard he thought it might explode.

Inside the shed, he glared at the gargoyle. He wished he could smash it to bits. "I'd like to scratch its ugly eyes out," Michael said. He punched the statue's shoulder. "I hate the way it looks at me!" His head throbbed. He punched the statue again.

"Cut it out," Sara yelled at him. "You won't solve anything that way. What's wrong with you?"

"I told you! I've got a headache," Michael snapped. "You'd be cranky too, if your head was turning into stone." Michael dropped his head into his hands and groaned.

Sara looked sympathetic. "I guess it's pretty bad," she said.

"It is," Michael said. He winced in pain. "I wish I could get Jonah Carter for this! Only he's dead. How do you kill a ghost?" he shouted angrily.

"Stop yelling," Sara told him. "You'll only make it worse."

"It feels like my skull is breaking apart." Michael bent over and grabbed his head.

"I never saw a headache that hurt so much," Sara said worriedly. "Did you ever take care of that bump? You know, from when you banged it on the gargoyle?"

Michael shook his head.

"Maybe I should look at it."

She touched Michael's head gently.

"Ouch!" Michael nearly jumped.

"Sorry," Sara murmured. She parted his hair and examined his scalp carefully. She patted it softly, right above his left ear.

"Is this where it hurts?" Her voice sounded choked, as if she were having trouble speaking.

"Yeah," Michael said. "It's really sore."

Sara's face had turned dead-white. She pressed lightly on the other side of Michael's head. "What about here?" she asked, barely loud enough to hear.

"Yeow!" Michael yelled. "Don't press so hard!

What're you trying to do to me?"

"Nothing." Sara dropped her hands and stepped away from him.

Michael peered at her more closely. "You don't look so good yourself," he said. He felt his stomach clench. "Is it bad? Did the bump get worse?"

"Not bump," Sara told him. She swallowed hard. "Bumps."

"What?" Michael stared at her. "I only banged my head in one place."

He frowned in confusion and raised his hand to his own head. "You're wrong," he told her. "There is *too* a bump. And it's really hard. And big. And—"

Michael moved his hand to the other side of his head. His stomach turned over. His fingers had touched another bump. As hard as the first one. And just as big.

Michael closed his eyes. He felt like he was going to throw up.

"You're right," he said. "These aren't bumps." He forced the words out.

"They're horns," he croaked. "I'm growing horns. Just like the gargoyle!"

CHAPTER 15

Michael began banging his head against the wall of the shed.

"What are you doing?" Sara cried.

"Breaking off these horns!"

"Stop!" she screamed, grabbing hold of him. "You'll really hurt yourself!"

Michael breathed heavily. He tried to calm himself down.

Sara spoke in a shaky voice. "We can probably file down those horns. Just like we do your fingernails."

Michael groaned. "I can't stand this, Sara! You don't know what it's like. I'm a freak! A monster!"

Sara knelt by his side. "We still have some time," she said. "We know a lot more now. We found out why you're turning into a gargoyle, didn't we?"

"Yeah," Michael answered. He searched her face. "But not how to stop it from happening."

He sighed deeply. He pushed himself up and went to the toolbox on a corner shelf.

"What are you doing?" Sara asked.

"Getting another file," he said. "To take care of these horns." He raised the file overhead and sawed it back and forth over one horn. It was awkward and he didn't make much progress. He made a face. "I need help."

Michael held the file out to Sara. She took a deep breath, then grabbed the file from him. Michael lowered his eyes. It was the creepiest thing he'd ever asked anyone to do for him.

"Sorry," he muttered.

"It's okay," Sara told him. She gave him a brave smile. "It's not that different from taking care of my pets."

Yeah, but I'm not a pet, Michael thought to himself. *I'm a human being. Or at least, I used to be.*

Sara started to file. "Remember, Michael— we've been in bad situations before."

"I guess."

"And we always got through them," she said. "Haven't we?"

"Yeah, I guess."

"So we'll get through this one, too." Sara reached down. She took his hard, cold hand in hers and squeezed.

That night, after dinner, Michael and Sara sneaked up to the attic again. They searched through the diary one more time. But it said nothing about stopping the gargoyle from becoming human—or stopping Michael from turning into a gargoyle.

Michael was getting stiff again. Sara helped him stash the diary back in its hiding place.

"The morning, Michael," Sara said. "Remember, you'll feel better in the morning."

Michael did feel less stiff in the morning. But he didn't exactly feel better. He had to get up half an hour early just to have time to file down his fingernails. And his horns. When he got to karate class, the horns had not yet grown back. Or at least not enough for anyone to notice. Michael nervously touched his head.

"Okay, everybody," Mr. Dooley began. "The exhibition match is coming up fast. Today is weigh-in day."

Michael gaped at the big scale that had been placed at one end of the gym. It was the kind of scale they had in doctor's offices—a tall metal thing. You stepped on a platform and a needle moved across a set of numbers to tell how heavy you were.

Mr. Dooley told them all to line up. Then he began weighing each of them and scribbling the results down on his notepad. Michael hung back at the end of the line.

"Max," he whispered, "I can't do this. I almost broke a ladder yesterday. I could totally demolish that scale."

"How can you get out of it?" Max asked.

Michael tried to think of a clever reason why he shouldn't be weighed, but he couldn't come up with one. Meanwhile, the line was moving quickly. Michael changed places with Max so that he was last.

"117," Mr. Dooley wrote down as he weighed Scotty Benson. "Okay, Tucker—your turn."

Tucker stepped onto the scale.

"124," Mr. Dooley scribbled. "A big guy."

Tucker stepped off the scale. He turned in Michael's direction and flexed his muscles. "Big enough," he threatened.

"Max, you're next," Mr. Dooley announced.

Max stepped onto the scale.

"101," Mr. Dooley called out. He wrote it down on his pad.

"Okay, Michael. You're up."

"Uh, you know, Mr. Dooley," Michael stalled. "Uh, I just weighed myself this morning. Ninety-nine pounds on the button."

"Michael . . ."

"I always weigh exactly two pounds less than Max," Michael insisted. "It's an amazing thing—"

"Michael," Mr. Dooley said. "Are you afraid of this scale?"

Tucker snickered. A couple of the other kids laughed too.

"Yeah, actually, I am afraid," Michael said. "'Cause, um, I put on a lot of weight lately. Trying to bulk up. A lot of weight."

"No problem. Step on anyway." Mr. Dooley was waiting. The entire class was waiting.

Michael put the front of his right foot on the scale. The needle started swinging crazily from one end of the numbers to the other.

"What the—" Mr. Dooley stared at the scale. "Get off, Michael. There must be something wrong with this thing."

Michael stepped off the scale.

Tucker and some of the other kids turned to watch. "What's the matter, Buckner?" Tucker called out. "Can't control your need to stuff your face?"

Mr. Dooley ignored Tucker. "Try it again," he told Michael. "And put both feet on it this time."

Michael gave Max a helpless look. Max shrugged. Michael took a deep breath. Then he stepped onto the scale.

The needle flew to the highest numbers and stayed there. A funny sound—like springs breaking—rang out. Michael quickly jumped off the scale. "Sorry, Mr. Dooley! I was afraid I might break it."

Mr. Dooley was staring at the scale in disbelief.

"I heard that, too, Michael. I can't believe this equipment is so shoddy," Mr. Dooley complained. "I'm calling the company, first thing in the morning."

"He nearly broke the scale!" Tucker laughed. "Hey, fat boy," he called. "This is karate, not heavyweight wrestling!"

"Okay!" Mr. Dooley interrupted. "To the mats! We've got work to do."

Michael paired up with Max. Luckily, Mr. Dooley didn't tell Max to switch with Tucker. The teacher was more concerned with showing them strategies today—different ways to out-think their opponents.

"Karate teaches us that size isn't everything," Mr. Dooley lectured. "You might weigh half as much as your opponent. But if you use your body wisely, you can win anyway. Focus! Center your energy. And *think!*"

Mr. Dooley chose Scotty Benson as his partner. "I'll show you what I mean," he said. "Scotty, you circle me. Wait for an opening, then make your move."

Scotty did as he was told. He and Mr. Dooley circled each other on the mats. Michael and Max moved up close to them to watch.

"Arrgh!" Mr. Dooley scowled and grunted. He leaned toward Scotty. Scotty jumped back. His arms flew to his sides, leaving his stomach and chest wide open. Mr. Dooley aimed a lightning-fast kick towards Scotty. He didn't connect, of course—they weren't supposed to hurt each other.

Scotty looked surprised. So did the rest of the class.

Mr. Dooley smiled. "See? That's intimidation," he told them. "I acted fierce. When I grunted and leaned toward Scott, he assumed I was about to attack. His instincts told him to jump. And he did—leaving himself wide-open. I could've had him then. All because I outthought him. I had him on the run." Mr. Dooley bowed to Scotty.

Scott looked embarrassed. He took his place in the circle of kids around the mats.

"Wow. Pretty cool," Max murmured to Michael.

"Yeah," Michael agreed.

"Okay," Mr. Dooley said. "Let's try it another way." The teacher glanced around the gym. "Michael," he called. "Our heavyweight—" There were titters of laughter. "You be my partner this time."

Michael didn't want to spar with the teacher. But everyone was waiting—including Mr. Dooley. Michael took his place opposite the teacher on the mat. He and Mr. Dooley bowed to each other.

"Watch now," Mr. Dooley ordered. He and Michael began circling each other. Mr. Dooley was in a half-squatting position. His eyes were glued to Michael's face. Michael kept his own eyes on Mr. Dooley's. *What's he going to do?* Michael wondered.

He was waiting for the teacher to trick him again. Mr. Dooley grunted and leaned toward Michael. Michael was prepared. He held his ground. His hands were raised, ready to strike. Mr. Dooley smiled faintly and leaned back. They continued to circle each other. Suddenly, Michael saw the teacher's eyes drop as he glanced down to one side.

That's it! Michael thought. *My big chance!*

Michael aimed a punch at the teacher. His right hand flew towards Mr. Dooley's neck—and was blocked.

Michael gasped. So did the class. Michael's arm was locked firmly in place by Mr. Dooley's arm.

"Tricked you, Michael," Mr. Dooley said. "I knew your position exactly. I dropped my eyes on purpose, to make you think I wasn't paying attention. You thought I left myself open—and you never expected me to fight you. Big mistake."

Big mistake is right, Michael thought as the rest of the class laughed.

"Don't laugh," Mr. Dooley warned them. "You'll be tricked too, plenty of times. Just learn your lesson. And be ready the next time."

Mr. Dooley paired them up to practice strategies. He made Michael partners with Tucker. They faced each other across the mat. Michael waited for Tucker to bow first. Tucker waited for Michael. Finally, they each bowed at the same time.

"Say your prayers, Buckner," Tucker muttered. "I'm going to waste you."

CHAPTER 16

Michael kept his eyes pinned on Tucker's. Michael was strong. Stronger than anyone guessed. He could probably destroy Tucker with one blow. But Tucker was mean. *Mean enough,* Michael thought, *that maybe strength didn't matter.*

Michael and Tucker circled each other on the mat.

Michael was still a little afraid of Tucker. *Maybe he knows a special trick,* Michael thought.

He started to lean toward Tucker, and saw Tucker do the same. They both dropped back to position. They circled again. Tucker drew closer to Michael. Michael held his ground. They kept circling. And circling.

"All right, you two." Mr. Dooley chuckled and pushed them apart. "Sometimes, nobody wants to leave themselves open. You'll have to try it again next time."

Mr. Dooley waited for Michael and Tucker to bow to each other. Finally they did. "Okay, class," the teacher announced. "Go home now. And get some rest!"

It began to rain as Michael and Max walked home. "That was a great class, wasn't it?" Max said.

"Pretty good," Michael admitted. He was surprised that he had enjoyed it. He hadn't enjoyed much of anything lately.

"I'll call you later," Max promised. "To see how you are."

Michael nodded. "Sure," he said.

Max phoned late that night, as he had promised. Michael had nothing new to tell him. He and Sara were no closer to figuring out how to stop him from becoming a gargoyle.

"At least my folks haven't bothered us all night," he told Max. "My dad's helping my mom load some kind of new software into the computer. It's supposed to help them keep track of their household bills."

Max snorted. "Yeah, like bills matter," he said.

"Yeah," Michael agreed. He promised to call if anyting happened. Then he and Max hung up.

"Don't watch too much TV," Michael's father had told him after dinner.

Michael hadn't watched any TV. Instead, he had sat in his room and watched his fingers beginning to curl. And his nails—they were going to need filing again soon. Not to mention his horns. . . .

Sara wandered into his room. Gruff was at her side. He bounded over to Michael and whimpered.

"Hiyah, boy," Michael said without any enthusiasm. Gruff pushed his nose into Michael's hand. Michael patted the big dog absently.

"How're you doing?" Sara asked.

"I can't stand it!" he suddenly yelled to Sara. "That's how I'm doing! We can't just sit here! We have to do something." Michael struggled to his feet. "I can't keep pretending to be normal anymore. I broke a scale in karate class today. I can't keep hiding how heavy I am, Sara," Michael cried. "Or how strong I'm getting. And we still have no idea how to stop this from happening!"

"I know, but—"

"No! No more buts!" Michael shouted. "We have to destroy it, Sara. I can't just sit here and let this happen to me."

"No, Michael," Sara argued. "Don't do anything yet. I'm telling you. It's a bad mstake."

Michael shook his head. "I don't think so. If it's getting flesh and skin, I *can* kill it, Sara. The more human it gets, the easier I can hurt it. I have to." Michael headed for the door.

"It could hurt you, Michael," Sara cried. "It has Jonah Carter on its side. You could be stuck this way forever!"

"I don't care!" Michael yelled. "I don't care!"

He plunged down the stairs. Sara followed after him.

Outside, the sky was pitch black. The rain pelted down on him as he lumbered across the backyard. Sara grabbed the flashlight from the kitchen and hurried after him. Michael went straight to the toolshed. Sara shone the flashlight on the ground to light their way.

"Michael!" she tried to warn him again. "Don't do something supid. Turn back. I know you're mad, but—"

"I *don't* want to do this." Michael swallowed hard. "But I've got to do something!"

Michael reached for the door to the shed. It was torn off its hinges. Michael stared at it briefly. "Oh, no—"

He ran into the shed. Sara swung the flashlight in an arc over the work table.

Michael drew in his breath.

The table was empty.

Michael and Sara gaped at it. "It's gone!" Michael finally cried. "Where is it?" he shouted. He raised his fist and brought it down angrily onto the tabletop. The heavy board split in half.

"Stop it!" Sara yelled. "Dad must have moved it already."

They hurried outside and around to the front of the house. Sara shivered as the cold rain pounded down on them. Michael didn't even feel it. He waited for his eyes to adjust to the darkness. He scanned the roof. "It's not there," he cried. "It's not on the base."

Their father hadn't said anything about moving the statue. And it hadn't been back on the roof when they came home from school.

"It must be in the shed," Michael insisted. "Maybe Dad put it on the ground. Or covered it up or something." Michael whirled and stomped furiously back to the toolshed. Sara kept up with him, shining the flashlight on the ground. Suddenly Sara stopped short. She grabbed Michael's arm.

"M-Michael," she stuttered. "Look—!"

Michael stared at the patch of ground that showed up in the glare of the flashlight.

There were footprints in the wet patch of mud near the door to the toolshed. Big footprints.

Footprints that looked more like claws than feet.

Claws with webbed toes. And long, sharp, pointed talons.

"The gargoyle," Michael's voice was a whisper. "It's been walking around." He turned to Sara.

"It's alive."

CHAPTER 17

Michael gazed at Sara in terror. "The door to the toolshed was torn off its hinges."

"The gargoyle must have done that," Sara said.

"But where did it go?" he asked. "Is it out here, waiting for me?"

Michael turned to Sara. He saw the frightened look in her eyes.

"Maybe it's gone," Michael said. "Maybe it just wanted to get away from here."

"I don't think so," Sara told him. "I think it needs you, Michael. And you're not completely a statue yet. So it can't be completely a human yet."

"You mean, we're the same," Michael said slowly. "It's turning into a human at the same rate that I'm turning into a statue?"

"I think so."

"Then maybe it can only walk around at night. Like I get the stiffest at night."

Sara aimed the flashlight around the back-yard. She turned to Michael. "What if—what if it's looking for you?"

"I'll be ready for it," Michael told her.

It was early morning when Michael waited by the toolshed. *Where is the gargoyle?* he thought as he scanned the backyard. There was a sudden rustling sound as something scurried past him through the wet grass.

Too small for a gargoyle.

A gust of wind blew against Michael's neck. He heard the creaking branches of the huge old oak tree that shaded the yard. Something was climbing it. Michael glanced up. A chipmunk scurried to the top branches.

The rain had stopped. But the weather was turning colder. Michael started to shiver.

Crack!

What was that noise?

Michael whirled around. A dark shape was approaching through the thick stand of trees at the end of the yard. He broke into a cold sweat.

I could run. I'm still a fast runner. And I'm not so stiff now, in the morning.

The dark shape drew closer. Michael's heart pounded loudly in his chest.

"Michael?"

Michael jumped. His heart did a back flip.

"Michael. It's me!"

Max! It was Max!

Max broke clear of the trees and ran across the wet grass toward the toolshed. Michael flung himself at his best friend. "Max, am I glad to see you!" Michael cried.

Max grinned at him.

"But what are you doing here?" Michael asked. "It's so early."

"What are *you* doing here?"

"I'm looking for the gargoyle," Michael told him. "It got away. It's gone—somewhere. I was looking for it, and I started hearing all these noises, and—"

"Noises?" Max interrupted. "What kind of noises?"

"Well, like, scratching noises."

"Yeah? Like this?" Max pulled his hands from his jacket pockets.

Michael gaped at them in disbelief. "Max—" he choked. "What happened? How did you . . . ?"

Michael's mouth turned dry. He tried to swallow. His eyes fastened on the ends of Max's fingers. Max had long, shining talons instead of fingernails.

Max dragged the talons down the length of his own arms. "Were the scratching noises like this?"

"Stop it, Max!" Michael cried. "How did—how did this happen to you?"

"Don't you know, Michael?" Max took a step

toward Michael. He raised his hands as if he were about to attack.

Michael opened his mouth to scream.

"Michael?" his father called across the lawn.

"Dad!" Michael yelled in relief. He started to run toward the sound of his father's voice.

His father ran toward him. "Don't worry, Michael," he called. "We're here."

Suddenly Michael saw his mother, standing next to his dad. *When did she get here?* he wondered.

"Michael, don't worry, honey," his mother cried.

Michael tried to run to his mother. But he was too stiff. Suddenly, he felt so heavy that he could barely lift his legs. He felt like he was sinking into the soft, rain-soaked ground.

"Mom—" he croaked. He was trying to reach her, but he couldn't get there.

"Mom," he called out. "Something happened to Max!"

"What about Max?" his mother asked.

"He's—Max is turning into—"

Wait, he thought. *Mom and Dad don't know about the gargoyle. They can't see it. I can't tell them about it—*

"Michael, honey," his mother was saying. "Come back in the house. Come in and get warm."

His mother reached toward him. "Come on, honey—"

Her hand touched his. Michael shrank back. Her hand was cold. Icy cold.

Suddenly Max was there. Max flung himself at the ground. He grabbed Michael by the ankles. His sharp nails dug into Michael's skin.

"No!" Michael tried to scream. "No!" But no words came out.

And then he woke up.

He looked around. He was in his bed. In his room. It was still nighttime.

A dream, he thought wildly. His heart was pounding. *Only a dream . . .* He tried to laugh. The sound caught in his throat. *My feet probably got caught in my sheets,* he told himself.

He glanced toward the end of his bed. And his blood turned cold.

The gargoyle was in his room. And it had him by the ankles.

CHAPTER 18

Michael opened his mouth to scream, but no sound came out. He tried to fling himself off the bed, but he couldn't move. He was too afraid to move.

This is no dream, Michael thought hysterically. *This is really happening!*

The gargoyle tightened its grasp on his ankles. It pulled Michael off the bed and across the floor of his room. It was dragging him toward the bedroom window, he realized.

Michael struggled to sit up, to reach the gargoyle's razor-sharp talons. But he wasn't tall enough. He fell back to the floor as the gargoyle moved steadily toward the window. The gargoyle grinned down at him—that same twisted grin it always had on its ugly face.

"Let me go!" Michael screamed.

Suddenly the door to his room burst open. Gruff! The big dog bounded into the room, stopped, and reared back. A deep growl started in his throat. In the next instant, he had leaped at the gargoyle. Gruff snapped at the creature's hands. He leaped up at the gargoyle's throat. "Good boy!" Michael yelled. "Get him, Gruff!"

Then something big and black lashed out at the dog. Gruff jumped away with a whimper.

The gargoyle's wings! Michael had forgotten all about them. The gargoyle might be turning into flesh. It was no longer as hard as stone. But its giant wings were still powerful. And they gave the gargoyle an extra advantage.

The gargoyle's wings slashed through the air. Gruff growled again and leaped back at the gargoyle.

"No, boy! No!" Michael shouted this time. "Go back!"

The nasty wings slashed right at Gruff's face.

"Go back, boy!" Michael yelled.

But Gruff kept jumping at the creature, trying to sink his teeth into it. The wings flew down and knocked the dog aside.

Michael kicked his feet, trying to loosen the gargoyle's grip on his ankles. But the talons only gripped tighter.

The gargoyle dragged him underneath the windowsill. Now it was trying to hoist him up and push him through the open window. The gargoyle grabbed Michael around his waist. Michael smelled its heavy, stale odor. He choked. But his arms could reach it now. He started pounding at the gargoyle's chest. Its soft flesh sank under his blows. Michael knew he was strong now. He had to be hurting it. But the gargoyle gave no sign that it was injured.

Instead, the creature flung its enormous wings around him. His arms were pinned. He couldn't move.

The gargoyle wrestled Michael out of the window. It pulled him onto the narrow ledge that ran the length of the roof.

Michael felt a blast of cold night air. His heart was racing. He glanced down in fear. The ground seemed awfully far away. Michael's heart pounded. Was the gargoyle going to throw him over the edge of the roof?

"Stop it!" he screamed. "What are you doing?"

"Michael!" Sara appeared at his open window.

The gargoyle relaxed its grip. For an instant, the cruel talons loosened.

I'm free!

Michael wrenched his ankles away. He threw himself to one side to roll clear of the talons. But he was heading right toward the edge of the roof.

"Michael! Look out!" Sara screamed.

Michael felt the hard metal gutter under his shoulders. Then he rolled off the roof.

He was in the air.

The gargoyle's mighty feet snatched at

Michael, catching his shoulders. The claws wrapped around him and dug in tight. The gargoyle gave a mighty leap. Its wings spread wide.

Holy cow! We're flying! Michael gasped.

"Michael!" Sara scrambled through the window onto the roof. She held onto the window frame with one hand. With the other, she stretched toward her brother's dangling legs.

"Sara! Go back," Michael yelled. He glanced down. The yard swirled dizzily below him.

Sara grabbed onto Michael's leg. She held on tight. The gargoyle beat its wings harder. It rose in the air. In another minute, Sara would be lifted from the safety of the ledge.

"No," Michael screamed at his sister. "Let go!"

He saw Sara glance down at the ground. Her face was white with fear. The gargoyle jerked its feet upward. Sara lost her grip. Michael's leg swung out of her grasp.

The gargoyle flew higher up the roof. Each flap of its wings sent cold blasts of air over Michael's body. He tried to stop his shivering. He needed all his strength.

Focus! Michael told himself. He struggled with all his might.

Michael gave a tremendous twist to his shoulders. *Yes!* He had wrenched himself free of the gargoyle's grasp. Now he felt himself falling. He squeezed his eyes shut as he plunged through empty air.

111

CRASH! He had landed on something hard.

"Oomph!" Michael pushed himself to a sitting position. He gazed frantically around. He had landed on a flat section of roof—a small ledge right below the third-floor gable. He was directly beneath the stone base. Right where the gargoyle used to be mounted.

The gargoyle swooped down at him, attacking him with its claws. Michael shrank back against the wall of the house.

A wing swooped at him. Michael threw an arm across his face to protect his eyes. The gargoyle swooped again. Michael lost his balance. He threw out his arms to steady himself. His right hand crashed against the stone base.

Michael felt a sudden numbness in his fingers.

My hand! Michael felt his heart stop for an instant.

His hand had been flung against the base.

Now it had turned to stone.

CHAPTER 19

The gargoyle swooped down low. It landed beside Michael on the flat part of the roof. Michael stared into the creature's eyes. He saw something new there. An expression that he hadn't seen before. An almost human expression. But without human warmth. An expression of evil glee.

The base! The base was the key!

Michael's hand had touched the base—and turned to stone. The gargoyle had fallen off its base. Jonah Carter's evil words were carved into the base.

> *Flesh becomes stone. Stone becomes flesh. . . .*

Michael struggled to free his hand. But his fingers were pinned tight to the base. He couldn't move them at all. The gargoyle was winning! The evil in the house was winning!

Michael felt cold sweat burst out on his forehead. His heart began racing in panic.

The gargoyle shoved its ugly face closer to his. It leered at him, like a bully. The way Tucker leered and taunted.

Wait, Michael told himself. *Clear your mind. Keep your thoughts still. Focus!* he thought. *Focus!*

An image of Mr. Dooley came into his mind. *Find the strength inside you.*

I do have strength, Michael thought. *The strength of a gargoyle—or almost.*

Michael concentrated hard. He forced himself to feel calm. He drew in a long, steady breath.

Focus your mind on one thing.

Michael squeezed his eyes shut. He tried to make his mind into a mirror.

Then the gargoyle lunged at him. Michael reached up with his good arm. He threw a punch straight at the gargoyle's face. The gargoyle reeled back. It staggered.

Focus! Michael told himself.

"Eeiiaah!" he suddenly yelled. With all his might, he pulled his hand away.

Yes! It came loose. *Yes! He was free!*

The gargoyle faced him again. Its twisted expression looked angrier than ever.

"Come on, Rockface," Michael taunted. "Come and get me."

The gargoyle took a step closer. Michael

noticed something moist in the hollow spot where its neck met its throat. Sweat. The gargoyle was sweating!

The gargoyle was almost human.

It might be quicker than Michael now. But Michael was stronger. He pinned his eyes on the gargoyle's face and kept them there.

The gargoyle lunged at Michael. Its arms reached out, trying to grab him. Michael twisted to one side.

The gargoyle stumbled, falling toward the base. Then, suddenly, the creature threw itself down and rolled away from it. The gargoyle fluttered its wings and rose briefly into the air. Then it landed on the flat roof again. Its arms flung out toward Michael—

Whom the gargoyle wounds, Michael remembered. *That's how all this started. So, all I have to do—*

The gargoyle's talons slashed at Michael's face. Michael ducked, but he stood his ground. The gargoyle drew back its arm to strike again. For a split second, it was unprotected.

Michael lashed out. His own sharp fingernails met the skin of the gargoyle's face. They raked across its cheek. Faint red lines appeared.

Blood.

Michael had wounded the gargoyle!

Now we're even, Michael thought. *It's almost human. And I'm almost stone. But we're even!*

Now it could go either way.

The gargoyle reached up to touch its cheek, feeling the blood. It whirled toward Michael. They faced each other across the narrow roof. The base was between them.

Michael was feeling more stone like than ever. More stiff. He dropped his heavy arms to his sides.

The gargoyle spread its wings. It was going to attack.

Michael drew in a deep breath.

Now.

"Eeiiaah!" He grabbed the gargoyle's arm, flipping the creature over his shoulder. It landed on the base with a loud thud.

"Yes!" Michael cheered.

The expression of glee disappeared from the gargoyle's eyes. Its face twisted into a snarl of fury. And froze.

The gargoyle was stone again. Every ugly inch of it.

It looked the same as ever. Except—

Michael leaned closer. There was something different. Three long lines marked the surface of the gargoyle's hard, gray cheek.

Scars.

CHAPTER 20

Michael stared at the creature. He couldn't tear his eyes away.

He felt stiff and sore all over. But this time, it was from his fight with the gargoyle. He raised his hands and stared at his fingernails. They were back to normal again.

He drew in a shaky breath. Very carefully, his fingers parted his hair and searched his scalp.

No horns!

Beside him, the gargoyle's eyes stared blankly into the night.

Michael thought about hitting its cold, stone face. Then he decided against it.

"Michael!" Sara yelled at him. She was standing at an open third-floor window. She reached a hand toward her brother. "Here," she called. "I'll help you."

Michael edged his way carefully across the narrow ledge of the roof. Sara's hand grasped his. Thankfully, Michael climbed through the window.

Michael's eyes locked onto Tucker's as they faced each other across the gym mat. It was the day of the exhibition match.

"What's the matter, Buckner?" Tucker taunted. "Afraid I'm gonna hurt you?"

"Think again, Tropowsky," Michael grinned. "I've fought guys a lot scarier than you." Michael suddenly dropped his gaze to the floor.

Tucker made his move. Michael was ready for him. Tucker's arm shot out a fast punch. But Michael's punch was even faster. Michael had Tucker blocked.

"Wow!" Michael heard Max exclaim from the sidelines.

"That's the match! You win it, Michael," Mr. Dooley exclaimed. "Nice job, boys. Now, exchange bows."

Tucker glared as he bowed. Then he stomped off the mat.

"Okay, Michael," Mr. Dooley said. "That's all for today. See you back on Monday."

Michael's parents rushed up to congratulate him. Sara and Max joined them. Michael's father clapped him on the back.

"Really good match, Michael," he said. He raised an eyebrow in surprise. "Hey! What happened to all that muscle mass?"

"Oh, I've got something better now," Michael told him.

"Oh yeah? What's that?" his dad asked.

"Strategy," Michael answered.

After a celebration meal of pizza and Cokes, the Buckners drove back to Moonlight Mansion. The car turned at the top of the long driveway. Its headlights swept across the front of the ancient house.

Mr. Buckner glanced up at the roof and started. "Wait a minute. How'd that gargoyle get up there?"

"Oh . . . uh . . ." Michael started to stammer.

"I forgot to tell you, Dad," Sara said, thinking quickly. "Those workmen came last night. While you and Mom were busy with the computer again."

"That's right," Michael agreed. "They put that statue up in no time."

"Well, I'll be. I thought they were coming on Monday." Mr. Buckner looked disappointed. He parked the car and everyone got out.

Mrs. Buckner gazed up at the gargoyle under the third-floor gable. "Well," she said, shading her eyes. "The old boy doesn't look any the worse for wear."

Sara and Michael exchanged a knowing glance. Michael gazed up at the gargoyle.

"Oh, no—" he cried softly. For a moment, he

thought there was a light gleaming in the statue's cold, stone eyes. Then a streak of lightning flashed across the sky. Michael blinked. When he glanced up at the gargoyle again, the light was gone.

There was a sudden rumble of thunder. Raindrops spattered onto the ground.

"More rain!" Mrs. Buckner exclaimed. "I'm going inside."

"Me, too," Mr. Buckner cried. "Sara, Michael —aren't you coming?"

"In a minute, Dad," Michael replied. "I just want to take another look at the gargoyle."

His parents shrugged and entered the house.

Michael and Sara stood silently for a moment. They each studied the gargoyle that was perched high on the roof of Moonlight Mansion.

"Jonah Carter won't be happy about this," Sara finally said.

"Jonah Carter has to learn something," Michael told her.

"Oh?" Sara turned to her brother. "What's that?"

"His evil might be strong," Michael answered. "But it's not strong enough to get rid of us."

Michael pushed the heavy wooden door open. Then he and Sara went inside.

Don't miss the other

House of Horrors

books

#1 My Brother the Ghost
by Suzanne Weyn

Sara and Michael Buckner have a bad feeling about their new house. It's not just the creaky floorboards, the strange noises, or the flickering lights—somehow Sara and Michael know Moonlight Mansion is haunted!

There's an evil spirit living there and he's trying to take over Michael's body. Sara must think quickly because Michael is fading fast. Can Sara save her brother? Or will the House of Horrors claim another victim?

#2 Rest in Pieces
by Suzanne Weyn

The Buckner dog, Gruff, is the best friend any kid could have. But Gruff has made a horrifying discovery in the backyard—something that's not quite human. And it's turned him into a ferocious beast!

Sara and Michael can't control him anymore.

The disembodied claw Gruff's dug up is scary enough, but when the ring it's wearing starts glowing, they know something is terribly wrong. Somehow Sara and Michael know it's alive!

#3 Jeepers Creepers
by Suzanne Weyn

When Michael and Sara discover a hidden room in their house, they wonder why it's been closed off for so long. Then they notice a strange purple egg under the bed. What could it possibly be? All too soon they get their answer: A family of horrible half-insect, half-rodent creatures hatches. They're creepy. They're crawly. They're killers! And they're multiplying fast. Can Sara and Michael get rid of the creatures before the creatures get rid of them?

#4 Aunt Weird
by Lloyd Alan

Michael and Sara can't explain why they get the shivers when Aunt Wendy arrives at the door of the Moonlight Mansion. Their new baby-sitter is very strange—so strange that the kids give her the nickname Aunt Weird. And creepy accidents happen after she comes to the house. Sara and Michael start doing things for no reason at all—as if they'd lost control of their own bodies! But

the real terror begins when Aunt Weird takes
off her head! Will Sara's and Michael's be next?

#5 Knock, Knock . . . You're Dead
by Megan Stine

Destroy the evil Moonlight Mansion forever?
That's Sara and Michael Buckner's most
desparate wish, and they'll do anything to make
it come true—even cooperate with a ghost.

But there's one problem. The ghost tells Sara
she must perform three tasks to rid the house of
evil. Unfortunately, the tasks are hideous
beyond her imagination, and they must be com-
pleted before the next full moon.

"Ignore me," says the ghost, "and the house
will continue to torment you. Obey and your
troubles will end. It's really very simple."

But is it? Can Sara and Michael really trust
their ghostly new friend?

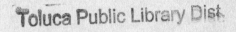